Edward Gilliat

Asylum Christi

A story of the Dragonnades

Edward Gilliat

Asylum Christi
A story of the Dragonnades

ISBN/EAN: 9783337274382

Printed in Europe, USA, Canada, Australia, Japan

Cover: Foto ©Andreas Hilbeck / pixelio.de

More available books at **www.hansebooks.com**

A STORY OF

THE DRAGONNADES.

By EDWARD GILLIAT, M.A.

IN THREE VOLUMES.
VOL. II.

LONDON:
SAMPSON LOW, MARSTON, SEARLE & RIVINGTON,
CROWN BUILDINGS, 188, FLEET STREET.
1877.

ASYLUM CHRISTI.

CHAPTER I.

It is said that sleep visits the fisherman's hut as readily as the nobleman's château; but Philippe and his father did not feel the truth of this saying when they lay down on Sunday night on two hard pallet-beds in an inner room. The cabin, which was of wood tarred on the outside, was built on a piece of rock only a few feet above high-water mark, exposed to all the fury of the wind from the sea, though sheltered by a high cliff on the landward side. It had once been a coastguard station, and was therefore more roomy than fishermen's huts usually are ; but the wooden walls creaked and swayed and groaned and creaked all through the night, and again and again the boy would start up and

rub his eyes, and cry "Qui va là ?" and his
father would answer " It is only the wind, mon
enfant, lie down and sleep again." And Henri,
who slept in another chamber, kept starting at
the sound of Philippe's voice, thinking, in his
half sleep, that it was Marie calling to him ; for
the voices of brother and sister were so nearly
of one tone and cadence that it was hard to
distinguish them.

But when the morning came, and with it
came gurgling and washing and splashing about
the windy rock, waves that were sparkling in the
slanting sunlight, Henri came in to bid them
rise and break their fast, for his pinnace which
was to convey them to the sloop was already
nearing the shore.

As Philippe stood on the verge of the slippery
rock, cracking the sea-weed beneath his feet
and inhaling tbe fresh sea-breeze, Henri and the
sieur were busy looking to the transfer of some
valuables which had just arrived in a cart.

"You will see that these are delivered in
London to the care of Monsieur le Marquis de
Ruvigny," said the sieur to Henri, "so that in
case anything untoward happens to me, my
family may have some means of subsistence till
Monsieur de la Bruyère can refund the value of

my estates in Normandy. And now let us to breakfast."

That day was spent in sailing to the sloop with the sieur's jewels, etc., and it was almost dark when they returned, for it was necessary that she should stand off lest suspicion should be raised among the guard that patrolled the coast; for at this time Louis had given orders that all the frontiers should be closely guarded, as it was no part of his policy to drive away from the kingdom the most industrious and prosperous subjects he possessed, as the Huguenots were, especially in the North of France. And to quicken and stimulate the capture of intending refugees, it had been ordered that the person who laid information against a fugitive should have a claim on half his goods. But in spite of this, thousands escaped through the connivance of the Catholic peasantry, who risked their liberty to assist those whom they believed to be cruelly persecuted, and Pelisson's bribes, which ranged from five to a hundred livres, for the conversion of heretics, produced but a scanty harvest. Converts were scarce, although they were exempted by a special law from quartering the king's troops for two years.

But to return to the fugitives. Henri had

strongly advised the sieur to leave Philippe on
board the sloop, where he at least would be safe
from all risk; but the boy had pleaded with tears
in his eyes that he might be allowed to share
his father's danger, and much against his judgment, De Cornelli had given him permission
to accompany him. The horses were brought
round to the cabin at nightfall, and Henri, who
was to stay in command of the pinnace, kissed
Philippe and whispered in his ear—

"Tell your sister that my life shall be for
hers and those she loves—adieu!"

And Philippe and his father rode out into
the darkness to meet the coach, turning as they
crossed the downs to look back upon the sea,
where a tiny light was visible, not far, apparently, from the shore.

"It is the sloop!" said the sieur; "she stands
close in for us to-night."

They rode on long in silence, stopping now
and then to catch, if possible, the sound of
wheels. The road was tolerably straight, but
so indented with hill and dale that even in full
moonlight it would not have been easy to see
any one advancing from afar, and the night
was cloudy, letting in the struggling moon-
beams only through occasional rifts between the

clouds. A village clock struck one as they passed a church some ten miles from the coast; shortly after they drew rein and entered an open shed which stood off the road.

"They ought to be here by this time," exclaimed the sieur, as he struck a light on his flint and consulted his chronometer.

Another half-hour went by, and yet they did not appear. The sieur looked at the priming of his pistols and sat with clenched teeth; at last a faint noise of horse-hoofs was borne to their ears.

"Philippe, ride forth and see who comes."

After a pause—"It is a single horseman, papa, and he is riding at full speed."

The sound of galloping grew louder; the sieur rode out and summoned the rider to halt. At this moment the moon shone out, and a mutual recognition took place.

"Why! Guillebert, is that you? is anything amiss?" cried the sieur.

"All is lost! Save yourself, sire; the king's troops are about!"

"What? have they arrested madame?"

"Malheureusement oui, monseigneur!" cried the farmer; "we fought while we could, but they were too many for us, and then they led madame back to the château. Constant and many another lie dead !"

" Poor Constant ! he has been a faithful friend —and Pierre ?"

" Ah, he killed his man admirably well ! At first he tried to drive through the regiment of dragoons, but when they shot one of his horses, he cried out, 'I am for living in peace and charity with all men; but if you want to fight, come on !' At the same instant he discharged his piece at an officer at five paces, and blew a moiety of his skull off; but, monseigneur, they were too many for us, these booted and spurred gentleman of the king, and madame begged us to desist firing, and stop further bloodshed, and then the rest were guarded back to the château. But I pray you return and get on board ship, for you are sought for."

The sieur did not answer at once. The ruin of all his projects and the death of his trusty servants overwhelmed him with grief ; at length he answered—

" I thank thee, my honest friend, for riding thus far to warn me of the danger in which we stand, and were I alone, to fly would be a duty ; but seeing that my wife and daughter are in the hands of ruffians who may maltreat them,

it is my purpose to return home. They will vent
their wrath, perhaps, on me, and leave the women
alone."

" But fear you not that they will send you to
the galleys ? "

" I fear it not, Guillebert ; they cannot prove
my intention to cross the frontier, and I hope
my services to the king will weigh for something."

Poor Philippe rode back with his father, and
never a song sang he; the little bird that piped
so merrily as they rode forth was mute under
this thunderclap of adversity, and his lip
quivered and eye moistened at the thought of
his mother and Marie in the hands of the
dragoons.

Guillebert pressed his seigneur to take refuge
in his farmhouse, which, as being the home of
a Catholic, would not be likely to be searched ;
but De Cornelli was determined to go home
come what might.

Soon after they had joined the road leading
to Avranches a party of dragoons was heard
advancing from the direction of Coutances.
The three horsemen leapt their horses over a
stone wall and concealed themselves in a plan-
tation by the road. The dragoons came by at a

hand-gallop; they were escorting a carriage,
which was closed round with curtains, and did not
observe the sieur ; but Philippe, as they passed,
thought he recognized in the faint grey dawn,
the shape of his father's carriage, and his heart
beat violently at the thought of those whom it
might contain.

It was growing light when they entered in at
the stone archway, but nobody appeared to
open the great gates. Pierre's mother had
evidently gone, for her windows were all
smashed in, and her furniture lay strewn about
the grass—an evil omen, that smote deeply on
the heart of monseigneur ! Guillebert left them
at the gate, renewing his offers of help, if ever
they should be thought of avail.

Instead of riding straight to the château they
turned off to the left towards the stables. These
they found crammed full with the horses of the
dragoons, which had been stabled three in a
stall, as close as they could pack ; one or two
long-legged soldiers lay on the straw, sound
asleep, and two or three empty flagons betokened the good cheer which had preceded
the repose. They took care not to disturb
these gentry, and rode on till they came to the
kennels, which had as yet escaped the notice of

the dragoons; here they stabled their horses, fed them, and made their way on foot to the château.

· The lord of the château felt like a thief stealing in unobserved; but unlike a thief, he found the doors all open, and valuables tossed about on the floor. A sentry stood in the entrance hall, leaning on his long sword, but his head was bowed upon his hands, and his eyes were shut; he snored contemptuously as they passed him by unchallenged. The sieur motioned to his son to step quietly, as together they ascended the great staircase and sought madame's private apartments. At the door they stopped and listened; all was still, but through the key-hole they saw a dim light was burning. They tried to open the door, but it was locked; then noiselessly they passed along the corridor to the sieur's dressing-room, of which he had the key. This they entered, and passed through into an inner chamber, which the sieur used as a study at night, and which had a door opening into madame's bed-chamber. They were surprised to find a fire burning on the hearth, and a pot boiling on the fire. The door leading to the bed-room stood ajar, they could hear the rustling of a woman's dress, as they hesitated.

"Jesus, have mercy on us!" exclaimed a voice.

It was old Mathilde, who had seen two figures in the gloaming, and knew not.who they were.

"Ah, pardon! c'est monseigneur, n'est ce pas?" she continued, shading her eyes with her hand.

"How is it now with madame?" asked the sieur, as the old nurse came in and warmed her hands over the fire, for the morning was chill, and her bones had been frozen with the long midnight drive.

"She will do now; she is in a gracious sleep, Jesus be praised!" answered the old woman, nodding her head.

"And where are the young ladies, Mathilda?"

"Oh, Sancta Maria! does not monseigneur know that they have been sent to Mont St. Michel? Madame, poor soul, would have gone too, but she was too ill."

"It is better so!" said the sieur, thoughtfully; "there, at least, they are safe from violence and shame; but what noise is that I hear?"

A curious kind of wail came from the next room as he spoke.

"That noise? Mais oui, monseigneur, c'est le petit!"

" Le petit ! Quel petit ? " asked De Cornelli, with a puzzled look.

Mathilde eyed her master from head to foot as a born ignoramus, and replied—

" Well ! I never did—no, never ! Is it possible, then, that monseigneur was not expecting another child to arrive ? "

" Quoi ! say you the baby is born ? "

" Aye, born indeed ! and as proper a little boy as ever saw daylight ; though, to be sure, I had set him down for a scholard. But he's no puny, he isn't ; he soon stirred himself at the rumpus them dragoon fellows made ; he roared as loud as the loudest of them. Aye, he's a pretty bit of handiwork, that he be !"

The sieur had not stayed to hear the end of the old crone's eulogy ; on tip-toe he stole to his wife's bedside. She slept, and by her side nestled a little being, fresh from the hand of his maker, all unconscious of pope, or Calvin, or Luther. He kissed the pale forehead, and beckoned to Philippe to come and see his new little brother, and Mathilde stood in the doorway grinning with unfeigned satisfaction ; then they all crept out again, and Mathilde urged the sieur to take refuge in the white tower, whence he could come out at night and visit his wife in safety.

"It is a good thought, gossip," replied the sieur; "let some trusty servant bring us food. I know where to get the keys ; but we must haste, for the morning breaks, and these ruffians will be about soon."

When Beretti had been locked up in the upper chamber of the white tower, he was still unconscious from the blow he had received in his fall, and when he came to himself he was a long time before he could make out where he was. A strange chamber, lit only by a very narrow slit in the wall, which seemed to have been invented for the purpose of letting in the cold wind rather than light, circular walls of stone, the absence of even a chair or table—all these things convinced him that he was in a dungeon. For an hour or two he paced up and down, pausing at times before the loop-hole in the wall to peer forth ; but all he could see was the swaying of the great cedar boughs, all he could hear was the rustling of the thousand leaves which fluttered thick below. As the night drew on he sang and chanted, sometimes shouted at the top of his voice. Once he heard a door slam below, and then he was silent, for he said to himself, "Surely they are coming to fetch me." They came not, and he sulkily

threw himself down on the hard floor; but not
to sleep, for the sound of wheels upon the
gravel called him to the loop-hole, and again
he shouted, but the crunching of the wheels
faded into the old dull silence, and with a sigh
he lay down again. He was dozing when the
sound of a trumpet seemed to ring in his ear.
He started up; the noise of horse-hoofs approaching in regular order was plainly audible.
Was the sieur calling together his tenantry?
Was he planning a revolt in imitation of that
of Quillebœuf? Again all was silent. The
Jesuit shivered; he was cold, tired, and faint
with hunger. Again he threw himself down, but
this time on his knees, his head leaning heavily
against the cold wall. He prayed, and the
angel of sleep spread her wings over him, and
weighed down his reluctant eyelids. The jingle
of a spur upon the stone steps outside once
more aroused him. With the energy of despair he shouted, "He hears me, he stops!"

It was the Sieur de Cornelli whom Beretti
heard ascending the steps to the secret chamber
in the floor below him.

"What voice is that, Philippe?" said the sieur;
"let us go higher and unravel this wonder."

So the two came to Beretti's door.

" Qui est là ? " shouted de Cornelli.

" C'est moi, le Père Beretti ! " answered a voice inside.

Immediately the key was turned in the lock, and the prisoner and the fugitive confronted one another.

"What is the meaning of this, Monsieur le Confesseur ? " said the sieur, in a cold and haughty tone, into which entered a secret note of surprise.

" Ask your *serviteurs* — ask your *maître d'hôtel* that question, sire ! "

" Ma foi ! He is beyond my questioning ; he is dead ! "

" Dead ?   Then what has happened ? "

" I will tell you when you have explained to me what you are doing in this tower."

" I have been incarcerated here against my will, as you very well know ; if you have come here to mock me, say so."

" To mock you—no ! I and my son have come here to seek shelter from your wolf-dogs —the dragoons. Perhaps you will modify your resentment when I tell you that we are, like yourself, prisoners in this tower."

" The dragoons here ! " cried the Jesuit, his little black eyes sparkling with joy and surprise.

" Then I will go and confer with the officer, and
you may depend on my good services for your
liberty."

" I crave your pardon," said the sieur, planting
himself in the doorway ; " it would be folly to let
you escape so.   On the contrary, we must invite you to accept of our hospitality, so long as
we stay here.   I will take care, monsieur, that a
chair be sent you, and in return for this you
shall write me out a free pass, stating that your
life is forfeit in case aught happens to me."

The father bowed and assented, remarking
that it was not likely the dragoons would allow
either of them to remain long concealed.   Then
Philippe, with his father, sought the secret
chamber below.

By this time many of the dragoons were
beginning to yawn and stretch their long limbs
and quit the damask couches or velvet *fauteuils*
into which as many as could had intruded their
muddy and blood-bedabbled forms.   There was
a savoury steam pervading the servants' halls,
about which were already clustered some dozen
soldiers, ushering in the day with a flagon or
two of red wine ; others were pouring in from
bed-chambers or reception-rooms where they
had passed part of the night, and were lounging

in the great hall, whilst the servants in their red
livery were preparing a substantial *déjeûner* in
the dining-hall.

In contrast to the green and yellow coats of
the dragoons, with their tall-pointed hats which
drooped over one shoulder, was the black cowl
and hood of the Benedictine, as he gesticulated
and out-argued Father Beauvais. The latter
gentleman, half feeling that his occupation was
gone, by no means looked cheerfully upon the
uninvited guests. And his zeal for the uni-
versal Church was considerably modified by his
regard for vested interests. His rubicund face
wore a puzzled look, and the constrained smile
with which he met the salutations of the soldiers
said as pleasantly as possible, "Sapristi! what
do you want here?" For Father Beauvais had
a round habit of swearing, and of swearing
roundly, when his ecclesiastical superiors were
out of the way. Upon coming downstairs, after
sleeping three in a bed with two greasy ser-
geants, who much incommoded him, he had
discovered from the *chef de cuisine* that a week's
provisions were being consumed at one *déjeûner,* and with the unselfish regard for his
patron's interests which always marked him, he
had indulged in some pardonable spleen on

the occasion. And now that nasty, prying, unwashed Benedictine was making a hubbub because Father Beretti was not to be found!

The more the monk shouted, and the more the priest held his stomach with disclaiming hands, the more did the idle troopers crowd round them; and when they found out that a Jesuit was missing, such a Babel of tongues clacked to statements and counter-statements, that appetites got themselves unaccountably sharpened in the process. And when the great bell was rung, but alas! no longer by the old *serviteur*, the venerable bell of the Abbey of Mont St. Michel—the dragoons rushed like wild beasts to their food, and the whole place re-echoed with the clatter of their spurs and long trailing swords.

How long the feast would have lasted it is impossible to say, had not an interruption called them off in the middle of it. Just when the cider and the gascon wine were beginning to loosen their tongues and make them ready for any frolic that might be toward, the Benedictine appeared at the door dragging in by the collar a poor mud-stained and bleeding prisoner, whose countenance was hidden by his large *chapeau*, which had fallen over his eye.

"Voilà, messieurs!" hoarsely shouted the monk; "I have brought you a prisoner who can tell where le Père Beretti is confined. Shall we put him to the question?"

A hundred voices shouted "Aye!" and all rose or turned round on their benches to look at the captive. A smart-looking young officer then approached, and tapping the poor wretch on the shoulder, said—

"Thou hearest what these gentlemen say? Wilt thou confess, or must we to the torture with thee?"

The old man lifted up his eyes, and with a hand pointing upwards replied, "The Lord is on my side; I will not fear what man can do unto me."

A loud yell of delight greeted this speech, for the demon of cruelty had entered into them, and they thought that he would prove obstinate enough to afford them good sport.

"'Entêté comme un Breton,' as the proverb goes," murmured the young officer.

Meanwhile a brazier of hot coals had been brought into the hall, and the monk, whose pitted face was now enlivened by a fiendish grin, ordered two of the soldiers to hold him down upon the live coals, which had been placed on a low wooden settle.

"And now, Master Pierre, it may be worth your while to confess," said the Benedictine, turning back his sleeves.

Poor Pierre no sooner felt himself seated on the brazier than he uttered an involuntary "Oh!" and tried to get up; but the soldiers held him down. A peal of laughter burst from the spectators. One or two women-servants had their apron-corners in their eyes, for Pierre had been a favourite.

"Oh! oh!" ejaculated the victim, writhing with agony; and beads of perspiration forced themselves out upon his brow.

At last one of the women, unable to contain her pity, burst through the ring of soldiers and rushed up to her fellow-servant, falling down on her knees before him and whispering, "Oh, for Jesus' sake, Master Pierre, confess where the Jesuit is."

Pierre pulled the woman close to him and whispered back, "Écoutez donc, the master's horse and Master Philippe's pony are in the kennel stables, and belike *they* are now in the tower. I fear to betray my good master."

"What saith the pig of a Huguenot?" shouted several voices.

"Find out for yourselves, cowards that ye

are, all of ye!" vociferated the woman, with clenched fist.

"Seize that woman!" shouted the monk, trying to follow her; but the soldiers, content with one victim, had made way for her to pass.

Twice Pierre asked for mercy, twice they allowed him to stand up, and twice when released he maintained an obstinate silence.

"Let the dog have some water," cried the monk.

And soon one entered with a pail of water, which they endeavoured to pour down Pierre's throat; but the old *serviteur*, weak with loss of blood from the wounds he had received on the road, fell into a swoon, and it became useless to torture him any further. He was carried out and thrown on the grass in front of the château.

"Les maudits!" muttered Father Beauvais, with a dark scowl at the soldiers, and knelt beside the fainting man with a cordial, which he applied to his parched and parted lips.

It was some time before he opened his eyes, and when he did, they were red and wild with terror, and rolled unconsciously; then a gleam of intelligence flashed in them as they rested on the familiar features of Father Beauvais.

" Did I confess ? " gasped out Pierre, wearily anxious.

" Non, non, mon ami ; confess ? never ! Thou didst hold out like a martyr of the true Church, staunch to the last ; and when they tried thee with the ordeal of water—les monstres !—nature came to thy aid and hushed thee to sleep, poor soul ! "

" The Lord be praised for all His mercies ! " said Pierre ; and the tears were rolling down his cheeks.

Father Beauvais wept too.

CHAPTER II.

WHEN the dragoons had made themselves masters of the coach in which madame and the two young ladies were riding, they turned the horses' heads homewards ; but a small detachment of troopers was sent on to get ready a light carriage and four horses from the sieur's stable. Among the officers who commanded the regiment of dragoons there rode a tall and handsome cavalier, evidently not of the king's troops, for he wore no uniform, but was dressed in black velvet, and the cross of St. Michael sparkled on his broad breast. He seemed to be of higher rank than the others, and though he kept himself out of notice, yet the officers kept referring to him for instructions.

When the lighter carriage, harnessed with four black horses, came in sight, the coach was stopped, and an officer requested the ladies to alight and transfer themselves to the "carosse," but finding that madame had fainted and was ill, it was settled that the two "demoiselles" should go alone. So Mathilde joined her mistress in the glass coach, and Ethel and Marie entered the "carosse," being reassured by one of the officers, who told them that their destination was a convent, and every care would be taken of them.

For two hours or more they both wept and trembled, as they recalled the fearful scene they had just witnessed, or pictured the terrible fate which might befall the others.

The leather curtains were fastened down, so that they could see nothing of the road; but violent jerks and joltings made them nestle together, encircling each other with friendly arms, and so, riding through the night and the grey dawn, they fell asleep. When they awoke, the carriage had stopped, the curtains were drawn back, and they perceived they were in a town.

"Welcome to Avranches!" said the tall cavalier, advancing hat in hand.

Marie looked at his face and recognized with a shudder the Comte de Pontorson.

Coffee was brought into the parlour of the

hostelrie, though it was still so early that few
were stirring. In a few minutes they were
again on the road with four fresh horses.

"See!" said Marie to her companion, as they
were beginning to descend the brow of the
lofty and precipitate hill upon which Avranches
stands; "see yonder star of gold glittering out
at sea; the morning mist is melting beneath
the new-born sun. Ah! the enchanted towers
rise, the gloomy rock starts from the bosom of
the treacherous sands!"

"What is it?" cried Ethel, straining her
eyes to look at what seemed an apparition of
an island rising out of the sea.

"Yon glittering star is the golden figure of
St. Michael which crowns the topmost pinnacle
of the abbey; yon rock on which the abbey is
built is the far-famed Mount St. Michael, the
smaller, to the right, is named Tombelaine."

Ethel gazed with a feeling of awe upon the
spot to which she had heard so many Norman
devotees had made a pilgrimage. The mount
at this moment was concealed at its base by the
sea-fog, which also hid the vast expanse of sand
which at low water rolls between the rock and
the shore. But the summit and the bluff precipitous crags loomed out black in the morning

sunshine, as a sudden flaw from the north-west
blew aside the aërial veil.

It was but a momentary glimpse the travellers
caught as they descended the winding road
towards Pontorson; soon they were among the
green fields, the orchards, and the sluggish
rivers which crossed the road to mingle with
the sands of the Gulf of St. Malo. But they
minded not the half-reaped fields nor the
squalid, emaciated, war-stricken peasantry that,
clad in goat-skins, crouched among the apple-
trees, or waded after fish in the turbid streams,
so strong had been the fascination of that weird
and solitary mount, with its legendary powers.

"Tell me something about yon wondrous
rock," said Ethel.

"I would my father had been here to tell
you, save and except these soldiers; but what I
can remember, ma chère, you shall hear. My
father says that in old time the mount was
situated in the midst of a vast forest, and was
called by the Gauls Belenus. On the summit
was a college of Druid priestesses, who used to
give oracular responses. Then the Romans
came, conquered, and called it Jupiter's Mount.
In the fourth century, I think, some apostles
from Neustria planted a colony of hermits there.

There is a legend about these hermits which my father says you may believe if you like. For my part, I think it very sad to call in question any of these good old stories of God's providence, shown to men so much more holy than any that live in our day. Well, you must know the curé of the mount had taught an ass to come from the village of Moidrey, on the mainland, with provisions, and to ascend with them up to the cells of the hermits all alone, without any one to conduct it. One day this ass met a wolf, that ate him up, and the poor hermits would have died of hunger had not divine Providence compelled the wolf to perform the duty of the ass, as the ravens fed Elijah, and the lions helped St. Anthony to bury the hermit St. Polpmier. That is the legend, Ethel, and I don't see why a wolf should not do what ravens did. Well, in the eighth century, St. Aubert, a bishop of Avranches, saw visions of St. Michael, who bade him consecrate the mount under his name, and build a church on the summit. The good bishop hesitated, and next night the saint again appeared, and placed one of his fingers on the bishop's forehead, making an indentation in the bone which even now is to be seen in the skull preserved by the monks. So at last the abbey

was built, amongst other miracles which I will
not trouble you with just now, especially as I
fancy I detect a sly smile lurking in the corners
of your mouth. However, you will see the
spring which they say leapt from the rock at
the touch of St. Aubert's staff."

"I thought I had heard that the abbey had
been the architecture of Satan," said Ethel, in
a tone of subtle irony.

"Ah! there is a legend—a very old legend—
to that effect. St. Michael and Satan both
coveted the possession of the mount; and
having one day met near to it, the archangel
proposed to him to build a temple there, while
he himself should raise another on Mount
Tombelaine, and the mount which we call St.
Michael was to belong to the one who should
build the finest. Satan, full of conceit, accepted
the challenge. In a single night he constructed
the abbey just as we see it to this day; St.
Michael, in the same space of time, raised on
Mount Tombelaine a huge palace, whose lofty
walls, transparent as crystal, shot flashes of
light around. Before such magnificence Satan
confessed himself vanquished; but his gloom
turned to joy when he heard the archangel
offer to make an exchange of the palace for the

abbey. On the spot he concluded the bargain, and took up his quarters in the palace, with all his infernal rout ; but what was his shame and confusion when, at break of day, the first rays of the sun made his palace melt away. The archangel had constructed it of ice !"

"Ha, ha !" thought Ethel ; "a very old legend, let us hope. Our English aldermen, methinks, would hardly deem his archangelic · reverence an honest man !" But she gladly saw Marie forget her grief in this new interest.

"As years went by the monks of St. Aubert grew rich and luxurious, got their services done for them by hired priests; so in the tenth century they were replaced by thirty Benedictines. Then St. Louis came from the Crusades and visited the sacred mount, and was so struck with its situation that he determined to make a military fortress of it, which was completed when Philippe de Valois established a garrison there. I believe it then began to be used as a State prison, and the dungeons and *oubliettes* were then constructed. In the fifteenth century the English, that proud but barbarous people, Ethel, overran all Normandy. With fifteen thousand men they came to besiege the little

garrison on the mount; but the besieged made
a desperate sally one day, just when the tide
was turning, and the water rushing in with the
speed of a race horse—as you will soon witness
—made the English retire so precipitately that
they left their cannons behind, and you will
see two which have been placed at the gates as
trophies of that famous day."

"And how came the Chevaliers of St.
Michael to be so called?" asked Ethel,
glancing at the order which was suspended
round the neck of the Comte de Pontorson,
who rode a few paces before the carriage.

"It was Louis XI. who instituted the order,
after a victory over the Duke of Brittany. At
the same time he presented to the abbey a
statue of St. Michael in massive gold. There
are thirty-six chevaliers, and when in full dress
they wear a gold collar adorned with silver
shells, and a medal representing the archangel
treading a dragon under his feet, and piercing
it with his lance, with this inscription, 'Immensi
tremor oceani.' My grandfather, I am sorry
to say, once joined in an attack on the sacred
mount—in 1577 it was. They were led by a
Protestant named Dutouchet, and got possession
for a time of the town and abbey, and the

souvenir of it which we hold is the great bell in the hall at the château——"

The recollection of home brought tears into Marie's eyes. Ethel kissed her.

" I weary you with questions, ma chère ; don't talk any more."

" Au contraire, it makes me forget my sorrows—I must not think of the present or I shall give way. Yes, after that the abbey was attacked by the Comte de Montgomeri, who tried to take it by bribing one of the garrison ; but I will tell you how it was done when we can see the spot itself—and see ! yon towers that rise out of the black trees on the left are the towers of the comte's château ! Jésu grant he may not carry us off thither !"

The comte had observed that his young charges were looking towards his castle, and as they were obliged to walk, by reason of a steep hill, he brought his horse close to the carriage.

" When mademoiselle was a little girl she did me the honour of a visit at yonder château. She forgets it, *sans doute ?* I fear the ladies will find St. Michel a trifle dull."

" Ah, non, monseigneur ! This is a time for prayers, and it will be some solace to dwell a while in a place so holy."

"Certainement! but one cannot spend one's life in such a fashion."

"I could!" sighed Marie, turning up her eyes with a pretty air of piety.

"Mon Dieu! I should brave the indignation of the archangel and storm the abbey on the chance of winning so fair a prize."

"But, monseigneur, suppose your fair prize should be unwilling to be won; would you use force to bring her to your château?"

"Ladies like a little force, I believe," said the comte, showing his white teeth and bowing to the saddle-bow as he spurred his horse on.

Marie was now greatly distressed for herself.

"After all," she thought, "he brings me here to make me his bride."

Ethel tried to console her, but she could not stay the flow of her tears.

They were now in the village of Pontorson. The comte was giving orders to the village functionary, and Ethel beckoned to the young officer who had accompanied them to approach the carriage. He did so hat in hand, and stooped to hear what Ethel had to say.

"Will you tell me, on your honour as a French gentleman, whither we are to be conducted, and under whose orders you are acting, monsieur ?".

The lieutenant bowed, placed his hand on his heart, and replied—

"When beauty is in distress the French soldier can do no other than render his aid. Mesdames, your destination is Mont St. Michel. This enterprise was originally prompted by the Jesuit Father Beretti, but his singular disappearance at the critical moment has left Monsieur le Comte, under whose direction we now march, the sole leader. Madame need be under no apprehension. The sisters in the abbey will be her best protection."

He was moving away when Marie put out her hand and said—

"One moment, monsieur ; to whom are we indebted for this frank kindness ? "

"My name is Lieutenant du Hamel," said the boy, blushing.

They drove on through a flat and sandy country, where nothing relieved the monotony of the barren soil save here and there a miserable hovel, and some conventual farm-buildings that belonged to the monks. Then the road grew so uneven that they were obliged to proceed at foot's pace, and at last they came to

the marge of that which called itself soil, and
began to cross the veritable sands—*la Grève*—
that shifting, treacherous sand which extends for
many a league around the mount.

The two girls had drawn back the curtains of
their carriage, and were looking with awe on
the sands which had swallowed up so many
brave lives. In front towered the huge pyramid
of granite, rising majestically five hundred feet
high. The desert of sand is cut by several rivers
and by an infinite number of pools of water,
caused by the depression of the surface, which
help on the rapidity of the rising tide. Here and
there long poles were fixed in the sand to guide
the travellers, and prevent them from falling
into any of those dangerous quicksands which
are continually forming along the coast.

Ethel never spoke a word, so deeply was she
impressed with the enormous mass of black
granite surmounted by gigantic edifices placed
one above another, and the solitude of the
sands, their boundless immensity, the low roar-
ing of the sea, and the barren coldness of a
nature desolate and savage, all of which shed in
her heart an unaccountable sadness. She shuddered, in spite of herself, at the lofty walls,
flanked by their towers and bastions; and the

tiny dwellings which seemed to hang on the
south side, where alone it was possible to build,
appeared to her imagination like so many
struggling flies caught in the meshes of some
monstrous spider.

As for Marie, though not naturally so brave
as her companion, she felt no fear at the sight
of the sacred mount, for to her it was a refuge
from the grasp of a man she loathed, and the
spot was to her endeared by many a miracle of
the olden time.

At the first gate the carriage stopped, and
a little crowd of bare-legged women and boys
gathered round; they had been hunting along
the sands for sea-snails and other small prey,
and their limbs were still red and their upper
clothes dripping with the salt water. The
Comte de Pontorson now advanced with two
veiled and hooded sisters, and commended the
two ladies to their charge.

" Hitherto," he said, " I have had the honour
of being your protector; I now leave you in
charge of the sisters of St. Michel."

Marie thanked him for his trouble and returned the salute of the soldiers, who were
drawn up at the gateway; they then passed
into the lion court, where stood a guard-

house and a few soldiers, whose duty it was
to receive the arms of all strangers who visited
the place.

The Michelettes, or heavy pieces of cannon,
taken from the English in 1427, were placed
close to the second gate which leads into the
town—if town it can be called—which consists of
a very few rude houses, built in the narrow clefts
of the rock, set off with tiny gardens, whose soil
has been fetched from the mainland. As the
four scrambled up the street, which was too
narrow for a carriage to pass, it was curious to
see the weather-beaten faces that thrust themselves out of windows on either side from the
quaint wooden houses. Now and then they
came to a side street, hardly large enough to
admit the passage of a man's body; then by a
steep and stony ascent they reached the ves-
tibule and the stone steps leading to the great
door studded with enormous nails.

One of the sisters here rang the bell, whose
noisy clangour seemed to awaken the echoes of
a deserted palace. At length the door creaked
on its hinges, and a Benedictine appeared and
received them into the guard-hall; thence they
ascended a stone staircase and found themselves in the cloister, whose triple row of two

hundred and twenty pillars, adorned with cor-
nices, moulded and enriched with a profusion of
fruits and flowers, called forth Marie's admiration. Ethel was in no mood to admire art
which associated itself with a prison-house ; she
already pined for nature free and wild, and the
grandeur of the architecture only struck her
with dismay. The two sisters still led them on
through the library, pointing with pardonable
pride to the vast array of manuscripts and
books which reached from floor to ceiling, and
out through a side door into the part which was
reserved for those sisters who undertook the
care and education of young girls.

A middle-aged, sweet-faced woman advanced,
holding in her hand a letter which she said she
had received from le Père Beretti some days
previously, instructing her to receive hospitably
the ladies of the Château de l'Esprit.

" But where is the other lady ? " asked the
good-natured sister.

" She is ill at home, and I would you could
procure me some tidings of her," said Marie.

" We will try, ma chère," answered the little
woman, smiling, and showing a sweet dimple in
her soft cheek.

Sister Gabrielle then—for that was the name

of the superior at that time—led her guests into
a refectory, where they partook of some simple
refreshment; and, as they had brought no
change of clothes with them, it was resolved
that the two young ladies should wear the
dress of a novice so long as they remained in
St. Michel.

After dinner they repaired to the church,
where they both returned thanks on their knees
for their safe journey; they then were shown
into a leaden court, or terrace, from which could
be seen a beautiful view over sand and sea and
shore. In front, Avranches, with its old cathedral, now levelled to the ground; on the right,
St. Malo and Mount Dol; far away over the
sea, Jersey and other islands riding darkly on
the gleaming waters of the gulf. They were
left alone here to their musing, and long time
they scanned the horizon on all sides. It had
been a hot day, but upon the breezy terrace
the sea-wind came fresh to their cheeks, rushing
fiercely against parapet and tower, as if dis-
daining to be checked by human obstacle.

"I had half hoped that Henri and his Dutch-
men might have rescued us," sighed Marie, as
she gazed at the receding cliffs in the distance.
"He was, I suppose, waiting for us on shore.

Poor fellow ! it will be a sad disappointment to him. Somehow, Ethel, it all seems to me like a dream, so much has happened in the last twelve hours."

The door communicating with the church again opened, and Du Hamel stepped forth, to their astonishment.

"Comment !" cried Marie ; "we thought you had gone away with your troop."

"Pardon me, we have got orders to guard the mount, so long as the Dutchman stays in the gulf, and I am much indebted to him for thus allowing me to enjoy your society," said the smooth-faced dragoon.

"The Dutchman !" exclaimed Marie, in surprise ; "who is he ?"

"If you will follow me, I will show you," said Du Hamel, and he led them to a staircase in a tower, whence they emerged upon a platform which commanded the horizon on all sides ; and pointing to a tiny speck far out in the west, "La voilà !" he cried, rubbing his hands with delight.

"And will not the galleys attack her ?" asked Marie.

"No, madame ; there is a truce between the king and William of Orange."

"Thank God!" murmured Marie; and noticing that the lieutenant had overheard her, she blushed and stammered out—"It would be so fearful to witness a sea-fight!"

"It is rumoured that there is a French officer with them," said Du Hamel, "and a strong force was sent off last night to intercept him on the coast."

"Vraiment!" replied Marie, assuming an air of indifference.

Half-an-hour afterwards she was again kneeling before the altar.

"Elle est pieuse!" said the aged monks.

CHAPTER III.

PROVISIONS were going rapidly at the Château de l'Esprit, and the king's dragoons were waxing fat at the sieur's expense. It is true some of them had been drafted off to live luxurious days, and to insult the ladies in the houses of one or two leading heretics in Coutances, to the indignation of the good bishop, who hated the king's mistress's plan for making converts; but there still remained at the château dragoons enough to consume three sheep a day and an inestimable quantity of the best cider.

Poor Durand had been taken in the skirmish, tried before the mayor, and sentenced to the galleys; his wife and Marguerite were sent back to the cottage, while Jeannette was packed off to the Hôtel-Dieu at Caen, an infamously loathsome hospital, as all hospitals were at that time, where the patients were allowed to wallow in filth and rot in vermin. It would have been kinder to have sent her to the criminal dungeons; but this little seven-year-old had offended the anointed priests of the most high God! She had obstinately refused to invoke the Virgin and saints, and said she would rather be a heretic with her dear father and mother. A heinous crime for a little girl, and one to be burnt out of her by the fire of suffering, if so be the God of justice regard this little matter with the same eyes as their reverences!

Three times the sieur had paid nocturnal visits to his wife's bed-side, and none were the wiser. In the day-time, to beguile the lingering hour, he and Philippe had sometimes played at lanz-knecht, or risked a few pistoles with the Jesuit at whist; for the father was more good-tempered now, thinking that all had prospered with his plans, and that shortly he would be at liberty.

Pierre had strangely disappeared, none knew whither; but his old mother had gone mad, and was constantly roaming about the house, and peering into windows with a ghostly grin, till at last the soldiers seized her for a witch and threw her into a pond, where she proved her guilt by floating for a minute or two, and the dragoons brained her with brick-bats, much to the general amusement. For it would be wrong to fancy that these light-hearted Frenchmen were actuated by malice in killing the old hag ; it was a mere want of sympathy, an inability to identify themselves with their victim—much what we experience in ordering the gardener to kill for to-morrow's dinner one of the chickens which we have been used to feed with our own hands.

"And how is the baby?" was always the first question of Father Beauvais when he came down in the morning. It had even supplanted the before inevitable, "And what may there be for breakfast?"

Mathilde, when she was spared for a few minutes from her lady's chamber, carried her head at a haughty angle, and gave herself (so the *serviteurs* thought) too many airs for one who had occupied so unimportant a position the last fifteen years. But the head nurse and sole *accoucheuse* of so proper a little boy felt she had received an accession of dignity, and was resolved to maintain it to the face of all who scoffed at her pretensions. Each morning when the barber called to know if madame would not be let blood, and when the

apothecary came to recommend his nostrum,
Mathilde put them off with a majestic wave of
the hand, lean and wrinkled though it was,
and assured them that her patient was doing
superbly.

"And let me catch a man prying about in
my lady's bed-chamber," she added, when they
had turned their backs; "par la mort! we
shall be as indecent as those barbarous English-
women soon, who indulge in men midwives!
What is the world coming to, I wonder!"

And Madame de Cornelli was so happy up-
stairs with her new little treasure, which she
regarded as an especial gift from the good
God to bind her closer to her husband! Old
Mathilde would get herself part hidden by the
screen, and stand with arms akimbo, beguiled
into a toothless ear-to-ear grin at the mother,
as she lay fondling her new-born child, till, in
the deep sympathetic joy of her heart, her grin
melted into tears, which trickled down her
withered cheeks into the corners of her mouth;
and thus she would stand till some sudden
shout from the boisterous revellers below, or
some crash of breaking china or glass, awoke
her to the sterner realities of a world not all
love, not all charity, not all perfection, and

she would hobble off into the ante-room and stir the gruel over the wood-fire, chaunting to herself—

> " Piller la veuve et l'orphelin,
> Faire la guerre sans se battre ;
> C'est être fils de Mazarin,
> Et non pas petit fils d'Henri Quatre."

And the mother, pressing a babe to her breast after so many years' interval, felt the old romantic love of girlhood welling up in her heart to him who had been ever a true and kind helpmeet, though the studio had often drawn him from his lady's bower, and Bacon and Des Cartes had weaned him from the once clear voice, the guitar, and the sonnet. So she stroked the little head on which the brown hair curled, and gazed into the miniature likeness of her lord, with such happiness at heart as only a mother can feel, and scarcely gave a thought to what was going on downstairs, heard with seeming indifference that Marie and Ethel had been taken away to St. Michel, was quite reconciled to the failure of the attempt to escape ; for she had her youngest-born crowing and nestling at her side, and into that little being and his welfare all her thoughts, energies, and prayers were absorbed—in him she lived and had her being.

On the third afternoon Madame de Cornelli
was dozing on her bed, her long yellow hair
loosely tied with a pale blue ribbon, the colour
of her eyes, when Mathilde came in to ask her
if she could see a priest.

"Who is it, ma mie?" hesitatingly asked the
mother; for recent events had made her somewhat cautious, even with regard to the shepherds
of the flock to which she belonged.

"It is Monseigneur l'Évêque, who waits
below."

"De Coutances?" cried madame, with anima-
tion.

"De Coutances, oui," replied the nurse.

"Then pray let him come in."

And the bishop entered, his dark locks now
sprinkled with the grey hairs of trouble; and so
long he stayed by the bedside that Mathilde
would steal in on tip-toe to see if her lady did
not look flushed and tired. And there she saw
the good bishop with the infant in his arms,
marking its forehead with the sign of the cross,
and she withdrew to a corner of the chamber
and fell on her old knees to take her part in the
baptismal service. And the bishop went downstairs again and looked very grave and stern at
the dragoons who were gambling on the great

staircase and drinking in the ball-room; and
Brother Francis, the pock-marked Benedictine,
slunk away from meeting him, and no one came
out to hold his stirrup when he mounted his
mule at the door. All (thought the bishop)
was sadly changed from the orderly and peace-
ful household of yore.

That night, when all was quiet, and the whole
house buried in sleep, except a few dragoons
who were playing billiards below, under the
influence of cider, the sieur again stole forth
from his hiding-place and crept cautiously to
his wife's chamber. She had been looking
anxiously at the chronometer by her side, and
listening for his footfall on the floor; and old
Mathilde, who sat dozing in the ante-room over
the embers of a pine-log, never stirred when he
passed her. After the first long embrace he
whispered to her as he glanced at the little
bundle by her side, from which came the regular and calm pulsations of human breath—

"So, my sweet has found her an argument
in favour of following Nature? Art sure that
thy instincts are not depraved, and of the Old
Adam?"

"Nay, mon mari; I know it is God's will
that I should give up all for the babe; I feel

it here," and she put her white hand on her heart.

"And what if thou wert called to choose between thy religion and the life of thy babe ?"

The mother did not answer at once, except by a sigh, then looking up she said—

"God will provide a lamb for the sacrifice. Oh, my love! it would be a fearful thing to be so tempted. I would give my soul away for the soul of the little one; but God would be angry with me if I were to peril my salvation to prolong his earthly life. Nay! what thinkest thou, mon cher ?"

"That thou hast spoken truth, as thy good heart always prompts thee when thou wilt take counsel of it and have none of thy sophistical confessors to tamper with thy womanly instinct. Verily, sweet wife, thou and I have much in common ; heart responds to heart, and thy soul lies in God as close to mine as this small hand of thine lies in the broader palm with which I grasp it. Dost not see, sweetheart, how the little pledge stirring yonder and burrowing with its little nose to thy breast has made us feel our unity of life and feeling ? What are our differences, being, as they are, logical and of the intellect, to our agreements in the great truths of

Christ, which we know and recognize rather by the heart, by natural feeling, which, through lives of self-devotion to high aims, we have kept if not wholly innocent and pure (a thing impossible to frail man), yet redolent of the divine spirit with which they grew in us at our Maker's bidding—eh, ma chère ? "

"We are nearer—I feel it," said the mother. "Yet I have been taught that our nature is fallen and corrupt from birth—— "

"Stay!" cried the sieur impetuously.

And the old nurse woke up with a snort at the sound of his voice, drinking half a pint of gruel in her confusion before she could collect her thoughts and mutter, "Poor lady! the master will arguefy her to death! Quelle bêtise ! "

"Stay !" interrupted the sieur, "that doctrine of original sin seems to me to be a one-sided view of God's providence. It is just the dogma of men who see half a physical truth and think to clench it by marrying it with theology. Look at that babe, divinely fashioned; no art of man has moulded those limbs, set the blood coursing through his veins (so we are taught by the English Harvey), or adjusted the subtle motions of his brain ; all that is there is God's handiwork. And God is all-wise, all-good, and in His wisdom, as groping in the twilight of science I fashion it out, He has formed us so that we hand on to our children all our tendencies, good as well as bad ; not bad only, as the scholastic dogma would seem to suggest. Hence the nature of one infant may be corrupt, of another weak and wavering, of a third sound and good, according to their several parentage ; and inasmuch as we all are imperfect, there are seeds of imperfection in every new-born, babe, but also natural seeds of goodness, handed down from our first parents. Now, the theologians regard this inheritance as a stigma, a blot on the race ; but I look upon it as a marvellous proof of God's care for man—an unbroken act of providence, or forethought, designed to help us heavenward, and to make us feel that we bear one another's burdens and live for our children as well as for ourselves. By this law a moral capital can be stored up for future generations, and so our sons and our sons' sons will be enabled to build on the foundations which we have laid, to begin where we left off. Ah ! it is a cheering thought ; it inspires vast and grand hopes for the future of the race !"

Madame de Cornelli awoke from the reverie

in which the low voice of her husband had steeped her in time to catch the last words ; she exclaimed—

"Mais, mon cher, talking of the future, what is to become of you ? How long will the dragoons occupy the château ? Something ought to be done !"

The sieur, recalled from visions of succeeding ages to such a homely subject as his own personal welfare, paused, rubbed his eyes, yawned, and replied—

" C'est vrai ! Something ought to be done !"

" Would it be possible for you and Philippe to fly to England for a time, leaving me here, where my Catholic friends will protect me ? In a few months, perhaps, all may blow over, or I may find means to rejoin you in England. Thou knowest, mon cher mari, that I would not propose this but to save thee from danger."

" I know thy faithfulness, my darling," said the sieur, kissing the little hand that lay in his ; " and I dare say thy counsel is wise ; yet it offends one's honour to run away and leave wife and child in the hand of the enemy. But who speaks there ? ".

This exclamation was caused by the sound of voices rising high in contention in the ante-

room. It was clearly Mathilde holding no
friendly conference with some intruder. Quickly
the sieur concealed himself behind the screen
which stood at the further corner of the chamber,
and almost at the same time the Benedictine
struggled into the bedroom with the nurse
clinging to his skirts!

"Madame!" she cried, "the friar will have
his will, though I tell him you are not fit to see
strangers."

"Sister" cried the monk, "I come to bring
the Holy Church's blessing, but this old hag
will have a curse out of me if she do not take
heed."

Madame de Cornelli looked from one to the
other, bewildered, and pressed her babe closer
to her breast. "What is thy mission here?"
at last she faltered forth.

"First, I would baptize thy infant, ere he
be spirited away; for men escape from this
enchanted house, no one knows whither."

"Ah! you are too late! Monseigneur
l'Évêque has done all that is needful, since my
husband has permitted me to have this little
one brought up a Catholic."

"Si!" hissed out Brother Francis, rolling his
green eyes about thoughtfully; then resumed,

" I have come, too, to bid you prepare for a journey to St. Michael to-morrow."

" To-morrow!" cried both the women together, in tones of indignation.

" Pourquoi non?" asked the Benedictine calmly.

" Pourquoi non!" broke in Mathilde scornfully; "get thee to thy monkery, Master Friar, and leave me to manage my lady. ' Pourquoi non?' indeed! Thou mayest be learned in the fathers, but thou hast been no student of the mothers, to propose so idiotic a proceeding."

" But suppose it be my will that she travel to-morrow, who shall gainsay me?"

" I do!" cried madame proudly; "I remain for the present in my own château."

" By St. Antony! thou preferrest thy husband and his religion! thou art scheming to cross the seas, and it is my duty to foil thee."

" What hast thou, a monk, to do with me, who am under the direction of the Bishop of Coutances? Thou knowest, too, I cannot move."

" Nay, I know it not, but would fain have some ocular proof. Allons! Madame de Cornelli, wife of the heretic, step out of thy cosy bed."

A shriek rang through the chambers; he had put forth his hand to uncover her. With a bang down went the screen, knocked over by the sieur as he sprang at the throat of the Benedictine. It needed a less powerful man than De Cornelli to overpower him, for the consciousness that he was surprised 'in flagrante delicto' had made a coward of him. They both rolled over on the floor, the sieur uppermost; but quickly disengaging himself, he grasped the fallen man by the hair and dragged him out through the ante-room, sending him with a kick down the first flight of stairs, using more energy than prudence; for the noise of the friar's bones rattling and thumping on the oaken steps had aroused from their bed three or four dragoons, who came half-naked, pistol in hand, to see what was the cause of the night's uproar. The sieur, finding his way blocked by these night-capped gentry, drew his sword and prepared to carve himself a road; but in a moment the flash of a pistol lit up the corridor. The sieur started, and all the blood rushed to his face. It was one of those moments in which you feel you are brought face to face with death, and are not sure whether you have escaped or no. The ball had missed

him, but the muzzle was so close that the sieur's
peruke had been singed.

"Yield thyself!" shouted the officer; "we are
four to one!"

Seeing that resistance was impossible, the
sieur gave up his sword, and was marched
downstairs into his own studio, which was now
used as a guard-room, and where he had the
mortification of seeing many of his most valuable books strewn about the floor, torn and
soiled—for the soldiers had pulled out a hand-
ful of leaves whenever they wanted some
wadding for their pistols—and here he spent
the remainder of the night under watch and
ward.

Madame de Cornelli had heard the report of
a pistol, and waited in an agony of suspense
until Mathilde, who had been spying through
a crack in the door, returned with her account
of what had happened. But she was too good
a nurse to tell her mistress anything but good
news. The pistol had missed its aim, and
monseigneur had escaped. Mathilde muttered
her 'Pater noster' to make amends for her
falsehood, and madame kissed her babe and
thanked the Virgin Mother for her intercession.

And the night wore on, and the morning

broke, and the château again resounded with
the echoes of the uninvited guests ; but as they
sat to eat their *déjeûner*, the talk was louder
and the gesticulations more vehement. Brother
Francis was the centre of a gaping crowd of
full-mouthed listeners, who came about him,
knife in hand, as they alternately cut off a
slice from the hunk of goat's flesh or mutton,
which they held in their left hand, or waved
their knives in the air to express the emotions
which their mouths were too full to interpret
aloud. During the meal, horses were brought
to the door, and the sieur was taken away to
appear before the Parliament at Rouen, as had
been ordered.

"Le pauvre homme !" said a young girl,
wiping away a tear as her master stepped with
drooping head towards the carriage.

"Silence, thou canting wench !" said a dragoon, striking her on the mouth and bringing
a stream of blood from her lips.

Two or three young dragoons ran forward.

"She, too," cried the first dragoon; "she is
a damned Huguenot !"

"Let us strip her and beat her," cried
another.

"Or try how she likes cold water poured

on her back for two or three hours," said a third.

"What you will," replied the first; "but remember the king's orders, 'Le vol est dé-fendu.'"

The poor girl was dragged away screaming, amid the hoarse laughter of the bystanders.

Philippe stole out of the secret chamber, anxious and amazed that his father had not returned; he tapped at the Jesuit's door, which he could not open, for his father had taken away all the keys, as well as that of the door communicating with the rest of the château. He told Beretti how they were situated, and the confessor shouted back his reply through the key-hole. It was like playing at confession, and both parties seemed like enough to suffer penance, if the sieur should have forgotten to mention their presence in the white tower, and if their daily supply of provisions should be stopped.

At ten o'clock in the morning the mother and babe were fast asleep side by side; Ma-thilde was seated in the ante-room, in the red arm-chair, and in her hands she held a bowl of pottage, smoking hot, which she had been watching on the fire with some interest, and was now transferring to appreciative lips, when, without any warning, a terrific blow was struck upon the outside panel of the bed-room door. Down went the pottage all amongst the ashes, and the bowl cracked and split into two pieces.

" Peste ! " cried Mathilde, running into the bed-chamber and finding madame sitting up in bed with wide eyes, and the babe screaming at her side.

" Ouvrez ! ouvrez ! " shouted several voices, and more thumps fell upon the door.

"What the devil ! " shouted the infuriated nurse ; " you will set madame in a fever if you go on like that. The door is locked, voyez ! Open it ? non, non ! jamais ! Allez-vous-en ! c'est moi, Mathilde ! "

The last words were uttered with a dignity befitting the sentiment. The old nurse had been so accustomed to bend everything to her will in such times as this, that she could not realize the fact that she, Mathilde, was nothing to the dragoons. She imagined that they must be awe-struck if only she stood upon the sanctity of her person and office. Alas ! her simple life in the provinces had not prepared her for what was to follow. It cost but a few blows with the butt-end of a musket to force the door, and then they poured into the bed-room of the agonized mother—a motley group of dragoons and priests and hangers-on. Amongst the foremost came the Benedictine, bowing with mock courtesy to the lady.

"So we meet once more, Madame de Cornelli, wife of the heretic! Thou couldst not travel, so thou seest I have come to bear thee company with a few choice spirits whom thou wilt find *bons camarades.*"

Madame cried appealingly to the dragoons, without noticing the monk—

"Soldiers of France, have compassion on my state! If ye lack money I will give you all I have, only leave me in peace, for Jesus' sake!"

One or two soldiers laughed brutally, but the most part looked foolishly at one another, as if they were ashamed of their doings. They were to be excused for that. They are new to this business as yet, and are not reconciled to doing the Church's dirty work; by and by they will warm to it, and we shall see no more feeble compunction in their faces; for this, like all other painful duties, grows pleasurable in the performance.

Meanwhile some of the dragoons had gone the round of the apartments, opening drawers

and pulling out lace and silk, for which they
proceeded to cast lots, as if the owner had no
more interest in it. Others had seated themselves in chairs, or by the window-seat, and
were puffing away at the tobacco, till the atmosphere of the room soon grew very disagreeable.
Madame lay quiet on her bed: her lips were
moving, but her eyes were shut; one arm was
folding the tiny limbs of the still screaming
infant, the other lay on the white counterpane.
Mathilde, who had in vain tried to coax the
dragoons to quit the apartment, now came close
to the bed of her mistress, and stooping, kissed
her hand. The soft blue eyes opened and
gazed with a glance of grateful tenderness at
the faithful nurse, and then the two whispered
together for a little while.

" I will send a trusty messenger to the good
bishop, never fear," whispered Mathilde as she
glided out of the room.

Cider was now flowing apace, and one or
two *bons camarades* had treated the company
to a rollicking song, which might have been a
cheerful performance to madame had she not
been suffering from a severe headache. The
baby cried louder and louder, thrusting himself more and more upon the attention of the

soldiers, who at first laughed at his ill-humour,
but presently began to curse him for a plaguey
little heretic. One sour-faced fellow stepped up
to the bed just as Mathilde re-entered the room,
and, touching madame on the shoulder, said,
with a significant nod of the head—

"You must keep that little brute quiet, or I'll
tear his tongue out by the roots!"

The poor mother cast a despairing look at
her tormentor, and hushed the babe closer to
her bosom. Mathilde, under pretence of ar-
ranging the bed-clothes, slipped something
shining under her pillow; her mistress clasped
the handle—it was a poniard. An hour passed
wearily by—it seemed a day to the mother and
nurse. At last the monk entered the chamber
again, and told madame that, as she refused to
renounce her husband, and since Monsieur le
Jésuite was still missing, he must take away her
child, for "*Sans doute*, madame knows where
he is concealed."

Now, unfortunately, those who had been made
privy to the secret of the white tower were
out of the château, and neither madame nor the
nurse had heard of Beretti having been placed
there, so the former protested with tears that
she was ignorant of his hiding-place. But the

heart of a monk knows only one mother, and
she of granite, or marble, arrayed in tinsel
and gold ; therefore tears had no effect upon
him. Rudely he tore down the clothes, and
was seizing the babe by the arm, to Mathilde's
horror, when madame, raising herself on one
elbow, wildly plunged the poniard into the
fleshy shoulder of the Benedictine. With a
cry of pain he let go his hold of the babe, and
struck the mother a severe blow on the face,
which stunned her, and she fell back unconscious.

The dragoons had crowded round, and one
said with a sneer—

"The she-fox guards her cub with sharp
teeth, Brother Francis ! What ! a monk turned
sportsman, and puts his hand into the vixen's
earth ! Ha ! ha !"

Another priest now took the infant in his
arms, and carried it, protesting with all its voice,
to the further end of the room, where was an
alcove, or inner bedroom, the floor of which
was raised a little above that of the rest of the
chamber, and upon this *estrade*, or daïs, a
blanket was flung down for the child to lie
upon. This was the ordinary place for the
bed, but the sieur had had it removed into

the more airy space soon after the notables
of the neighbourhood had crowded into the
ruelles or spaces between the bed and wall,
to visit madame *au lit* when she first came
from Paris as a young bride, for such was the
etiquette of the time.

Mathilde had hovered about the poor little
infant, and made it as comfortable upon the
floor as she could ; and though she looked un-
utterable things at the dragoons, who were
carousing and singing and shouting all at once,
she dared not taunt them any more, lest a worse
thing should happen. The priest who watched
beside the baby would not allow her to take it
up in her arms, nor in any way touch it, and
so she was compelled to sit an idle and helpless
spectator of its struggles and convulsed features.

The monk re-entered the room before
madame had regained her senses, and, being
somewhat frightened at the result of the blow
which he had given her, began to excuse himself to the others, saying that it was entirely
in self-defence, for in another moment the she-
devil would have plunged the steel in his heart.

"Heart?" shouted one of the dragoons;
"why, methought thou wast all paunch!"

"If thou art insolent to me," replied the

Benedictine, turning round furiously, " I will report thy conduct to Monsieur le Capitaine! Ha! she wakes!"

Madame de Cornelli opened her eyes and stared round vacantly; then, as the reality gleamed into her vision, she started up to seek her babe.

"Le voici, madame, fear not!" cried Mathilde from the further end of the room; and she pointed to the babe at her feet, who had now ceased to cry, being overpowered by fatigue; but in his slumbers such a heavy double-sob would shake his little frame as on a calm day throbs the rolling surf upon the quivering shingle.

And another hour passed by, and yet another, and once more nature, seeking for food, lifted up her voice.

"May I not feed my babe?" cried the mother.

The monk shook his head. " Nay, shouldst thou confess where le père lies hid thou deservest to be punished for thy malice to me."

Mathilde could not brook to look upon the child and bear it no help. She got up and walked into the ante-room, where she indulged in a good old-fashioned cry, uttering prayers

and curses between her teeth. Then she be-
thought her of her mistress, and carried to her
bedside a cup of posset; but the unhappy
woman refused to drink, and begged to be
left alone, and Mathilde's face fell all at once,
and she burst into tears all over the posset.
Then the dinner-bell rang and hope leapt up,
for the dragoons hurried away to fill their
stomachs. But alas, for the mother! the monk
and the priest remained at their post. Madame
beckoned to Mathilde, and whispered—

"For the sake of pity, run, fetch some trusty
servants, and let them seize these swine while
the dragoons are away!"

Off hobbled Mathilde to satisfy her mistress, but she knew that it was a hopeless
mission, for not a servant in the château dare
help the lady in her hour of need.

The monk presently looked up from his plate
of sausages, which had just been brought to
him, and observed mildly—

"In case there is any attempt at resistance,
it may be as well to inform you that I stamp
my foot immediately on the child's skull!"

Madame shuddered.

Amongst other ideas which occurred to Mathilde as likely to serve her mistress was that

of getting the mastiff to tackle his old opponent, the monk, but from one of the servants she ' learnt that Maintenon had gone away when his master rode to the sea-shore, and had not returned.

Another hour passed, and the chamber was once more crowded with the dragoons, who made a terrible din with their wagering and swearing and quarrelling and rattling of dice. Father Beauvais came in, looking much ashamed, and explained to madame how shocked he was at all that was happening. He tried to comfort her by saying that her innocence would come out in the end, and hers would be a martyr's crown. As he spoke, the face of the lady had flushed, her eyes gleamed with a strange brilliancy, she was muttering incoherently.

" Ah! the fever, the fever!" cried Mathilde, wringing her hands piteously.

Father Beauvais walked away; as he passed an officer of the regiment, he remarked—

" Monsieur le Capitaine, you and your brother officers will be held responsible if this Catholic lady should die; already she hath fever."

The officer bowed, stroked his smoothly-shaven cheek, then sauntered towards the monk.

"What think you, père; hath not the poor lady been punished enough? They tell me she is a good Catholic—we must take care."

"Oh, pas du tout!" replied Brother Francis, "the lady is, or pretends to be, a Catholic, but she has connived at her husband's escape, refuses to separate herself from her heretical family, and, moreover, has tried to kill me; non, non, mon ami, it is an extremely bad case, foi d'honneur! I believe she has killed le Père Beretti!"

"Parbleu! a very vixen of a woman, by your account!"

The officer went downstairs and ordered a fresh bottle of *vin rouge*.

At four o'clock in the afternoon baby had given up the contest with the dragoons as to which could make the most noise. His little neck no longer swelled with full-blown clarion cries— a feeble, pitiable wail was only heard between the pauses in conversation. It was no longer noticed; but Mathilde fell on her face upon the floor, sobbing as if her heart would break. She could not bear to hear the thin weak voice that spoke so piteously of pain to her motherly heart; and she lay and sobbed till, sore spent with watching, she sank into a sudden sleep.

But the mother, sitting up in her bed and tossing her arms wildly, kept muttering incoherent words.

"Poor lady!" said one dragoon, turning to look at her. "Aye 'tis a pity, François; see how white her skin is."

"It is marvellous pretty flesh, indeed! But cover the poor thing up, for she hath lost her modesty."

Five o'clock struck, and old Mathilde awoke. Glancing towards the babe, she saw that the monk who watched it was nodding with closed eyes. The afternoon sun, streaming through the western window, had long been imprinting on his back the gules and bars and other heraldic signs emblazoned in the centre of the windowpanes, and the heat had made him drowsy. Mathilde rose from the floor to fetch some milk, in the hope of being able to convey it surreptitiously to the child; but as she passed the bed of her mistress, and saw how the fever was rising and making havoc with her mind, she stayed awhile to minister such alleviations as she could, then sought the milk-bottle in the ante-room, and crept back cautiously to the whimpering anatomy of humanity in the alcove.

The little unfortunate had barely got a taste

of his food when a drunken soldier, wearing his red jacket on one shoulder only, while the other sleeve dangled behind his back, came up and snatched the bottle away, applied it with a knowing wink to his own lips—thinking, in his senseless humour, that it was wine—then, with a " Faugh ! " threw it on the ground. One of his comrades, merrily inebriate, picked it up and poured the contents down the Benedictine's neck, amidst inextinguishable laughter, in which the most grave could not help joining, when the monk started up suddenly in a paroxysm of alarm, and began reciting his " Ave Maria " as if his last moment had come.

But there was one who did not join in the laugh, one to whom the loss of that tiny measure of milk was fraught with suffering; and Mathilde, as she bent over the famishing babe, saw with surprise that tear-drops trickled prematurely from his eyes.

" Hélas ! " she murmured to herself; " then he will not live ! Already his face grows old and pinched ; he looks now just as I saw his grandfather look the night before he died."

And six o'clock was counted by the timepiece, and once more the chamber was well nigh deserted, as the dragoons went down to

supper. And when they returned at seven, they
found the lady singing so sweetly and calmly
the vesper service that they stood amazed.
Mathilde, with her finger to her lips, whispered,
" Hush ! the poor lady believes she is in
Heaven with her babe." And a sudden awe
held those rude and superstitious men of blood
as they listened to her voice, now climbing to its
sweetest upper notes, now sinking melodiously
to mellow depths of liquid clearness.

But the shadows of night came on apace, and
somehow the outward dulness of the chamber
seemed to influence the mind of the poor fever-
stricken woman ; for while the slant rays of the
evening sun lit up her face, she was in heavenly
company, but after sunset, when all her room
lay in shadow and gloom, she thought herself
in purgatory. At eight o'clock she murmured
Mathilde's name, and the old nurse, who was
ever flitting from the mother to the child, heard
her and stooped to listen ; but there was so
much noise in the chamber it was difficult to
hear.

" Will he come, ma mie ? "

" Who, chère madame ? "

" Lui, Claude Auvie de Coutances ; you sent
for him, is it not so ? "

"Oui, oui, parfaitement: he should already be here."

"I hope he will come soon—I shall die without the sacrament! How is le pauvre enfant?"

"Restez tranquille, madame; all will yet be well."

At this moment the Benedictine thrust his presence in and said—

"Now, madame, I give you your choice: swear to renounce monsieur votre mari as a cursed heretic, and I will give you back your son."

Madame turned her weary eyes upon the monk. "I am dying; tempt me not. Poor little one! Holy Virgin support me! No, I will not renounce my husband, God helping me!" and she sank back exhausted. And lights were brought in, and musical instruments made dissonant sounds in the sick-chamber until near midnight.

"Tell him that I loved him," in one of her lucid moments Madame de Cornelli whispered to Mathilde; "take this ring from my finger—pull; there!—give it him. Ah, it is hard to die and leave the little motherless babe!"

Mathilde slipped the ring into her bosom for safety.

The dragoons were getting very noisy, quarrelling and fighting, when an officer rushed into the room shouting "Silence!" At the same time a trampling of feet was heard upon the staircase; all eyes were directed to the door, where now appeared the white robes of priests, and the Host, borne beneath a silken canopy, and then the stately figure of the Bishop of Coutances. The dragoons sank on their knees and uncovered; the priests paced in two and two, and arranged themselves about the bed. The bishop asked a few hurried questions of Mathilde, whom he directed to bring the babe, hungry and cold, and lay him in his mother's bosom. This was done, but the lady was scarcely conscious; then the sacrament was administered, and for a long time they stood round her bed chanting, in low tones, a beautiful hymn. Slowly, at length, her eyes opened, and rested on the bishop.

"Enfin! c'est Claude!"

The bishop, who had known her and played with her when boy and girl together, now stooped and kissed her forehead, and as he did so a hot tear fell upon her face.

"Weep not, mon ami," she said, "I am going to the Father of all."

"Nay!" answered monseigneur; "you must live and nourish your little one—voyez, ma chère!" and he drew her attention to the little breathing bundle by her side.

Taken by surprise, she seized the baby and covered him with caresses, crying with extravagant joy. The nurse tried to soothe her, but the spring of tears had been touched, and none could stay their flow. There was no responsive utterance from the little throat which in the morning had sung out so loudly, only a faint and feeble gasping for breath, and when the mother noticed this she essayed to lift him to her side, but was too weak. Mathilde put the famished babe tenderly on her arm. The parted lips, however, refused to do their work; silent and motionless he lay, while all around stood waiting in suspense. The mother felt, with a thrill of anguish, that the little cheek was cold upon her breast; she put her lips to his mouth, there was no flutter of breath; she pressed his side, no pulsation of the heart was noticeable; then, with a scream of despair which rang through the whole wing of the building, she started up and fell back on her pillow a corpse!

Down on his knees, beside the body of his friend, sank the bishop, sobbing like a woman

for very grief; down, too, dropped the priests;
and the dragoons—those, at least, who had not
slunk away before—covered their faces with
their hands in the presence of Death.

When at last the bishop rose, and made
inquiry into the circumstances, he commanded
Brother Francis to be sent for. Candles were
lit and placed about the bed, at the foot of
which remained two priests, repeating prayers
for the souls of the dead—the mother and the
babe at her side. Then the door was shut, and
a guard was set to prevent any from entering.

Though diligent search was made, nothing
was seen of the Benedictine; he had fled at
the arrival of the bishop.

The next day, by order of Monseigneur
l'Évêque, the body was removed to Coutances,
in preparation for a great funeral in the
Cathedral. The cause of her death was hushed
up, and the dragoons were quickly removed to
another district. Yet rumours got abroad, and
the peasantry—for whom Madame de Cornelli
had laboured so piously—came clattering in
their *sabots* to honour the procession, and it
would have been a perilous matter for the
Benedictine to have shown his head amongst
them.

And so the Huguenots at Coutances were
saved for a time from molestation ; for even the
Catholics themselves confessed that cruelty in-
flicted on a lady of the faith, for cleaving to her
husband, did not tend " ad majorem Dei
gloriam." And everybody kept asking, " Où
donc est le Père Beretti ? "

CHAPTER IV.

LIFE in the fortress-abbey of Mont St. Michel
was somewhat monotonous to young ladies
accustomed to the exercise of the field. For
two or three days they were interested enough
in walking round the battlements, or climbing
to the topmost stair and leaning on a pinnacle
to scan the wide reach of sea and shore ; or
they would pace with linked arms in the *promenoir*, through the cloisters, talking much of
the past and hoping much of the future, or they
would visit with one of the sisters some bedridden *montois*, and listen to tales of hardship
and distress. The sister-superior had given
them a little room in which they slept together,
and their meals they took with the sisters in
common, one of whom always accompanied
them when they left the precincts of the abbey ;
but though Sister Gabrielle was always ex-

tremely kind and thoughtful towards them, she was so much occupied with her prayers and studies that they did not see so much of her as they could have wished.

One day Ethel proposed that they should examine the library, as a storm of wind and rain prevented them from walking on the walls. " They say, Marie, that is one of the most valuable libraries in France ; so that some call this spot 'the city of books.'"

Marie assented with a sigh. Her mind was too full of anxiety to care much for books just now. She had just heard that her father had been taken to Rouen; she feared for her mother and Philippe ; and her heart sank when she thought of Henri's danger.

However, they sauntered among the piles of old books and manuscripts, passing from one choice gallery to another like two butterflies from flower to flower, and there they found Sister Gabrielle seated in a nook by a window reading a great book. She rose at their approach ; Marie curtseyed.

" One of the fathers of our Church, Sister Gabrielle ? "

" No, mademoiselle," the other replied, blushing and hesitating; "I was reading the 'Gorgias'

of Plato. We are, you understand, here in retreat, and I take the opportunity of this leisure
time to cultivate the sages of·old time."

As the sister spoke a man approached ·laden
with two huge tomes that filled both his arms.
He was an ecclesiastic, though negligently
dressed, and wore spectacles, which were now
lifted across his forehead.

"A very learned man—an abbé. You may
have heard of his name——"

The sister's introduction was interrupted by
Marie rushing forward and crying out—

"Comment! is it you, Monsieur l'Abbé?"

The Abbé Huet, for it was he, stopped and
peered through his dim eyes at the impulsive
novice, but did not recognize her.

"You forget, then, Marie de Cornelli!" cried
the girl, making a mock curtsey before the
scholar.

"Ah! Mon Dieu! is it possible?" and he
hastened to put down his volumes reverently
on a desk, and took Marie by both hands,
repeating over and over, "Is it possible?"
And then he heard her story, sympathizing
deeply, yet seemed delighted, as he looked from
one girlish face to the other, that chance had
given him such fair companions. "We will

walk together on the sands, quelle joie!" And he rubbed his hands together with delight at the prospect of enjoying their society.

"Now I shall leave you to Monseigneur l'Évêque," said Sister Gabrielle, going.

"L'Évêque? Can it be true that you, sir, are promoted to that dignity?"

"Only . designate, Marie, of Soissons; but I am here to enjoy the sea and the books and the society of yon learned lady."

"Is she so learned? And who may she be?" asked Marie.

"Do you not know, then? She is the celebrated Abbess of Fontevraud, Marie Magdalene Gabrielle de Rochechouart, the daughter of the Duke of Mortemar, and sister of Madame de Montespan!"

"Vraiment! and she looks so good, too!" The tone of surprise in which this was said made Huet laugh.

"Evidently mademoiselle thinks that learning and virtue are two dogs that are seldom coupled," he said to Ethel.

"If the Abbé Huet were not also bishopdesignate, I could rally him on the subjects he studies during his retreat!" rejoined Marie, archly glancing at the man of letters.

"I do not profess to sit in sackcloth and ashes studying profitless teachers. Come with me, young ladies, and I will show you my ocean garden." And he led them through the friars' quarters and out through a window, as it were, in the rock, upon a little terrace, shut in on all sides, save that fronting the west and the sea, by boulders of rock.

Ethel and Marie could not resist exclaiming aloud in admiration of the art which had planted in so wild a recess such beautiful plants, in the midst of which a tiny fountain scattered its silver spray.

"Here," said the philosopher, "we economize space. The purple-orchis and wild-succory there I use to flavour our monkish pottage withal; then there are cresses and wood-sorrel to my *déjeûner*, and salep for my hot evening mess. Here I grow camomile to ease my toothache, and there buttercup, whose juice clears the head *by sneezing;* that is woodruff, excellent for the liver; yon poppy puts me to sleep, thyme gives me pleasant dreams, and rosemarie puts me in mind of old friendship. Now what lack I, fair mistress?"

"I see nought here that will keep you awake should you become tedious and drowsy," said Marie maliciously.

" Pardon ! I have the leaves of a rare plant
from China which the merchants call 'tea,' a
glass of which is a wonderful specific against
your untimely sleepfulness ; though, to say .
truth, I can sit up all night over my studies,
and come forth quite fresh next morning ! But
step this way and I will give you a taste of
this Chinese beverage, which I assure you is
much affected of late by the learned."

As they followed him into his little sanctum,
Marie observed—

" Tiresome man ! it is impossible to get the
better of him ! And such a naïve egotism !
Heaven grant this same 'tea' be not an
emetic ! "

There is no need to tell how Ethel and
Marie drank their first bowl of tea ; how they
praised it but coldly, yet tried a second and
liked it better ; and how afterwards they always
came in the evening and mixed for the abbé
his Chinese tea-drink, and never failed to quaff
a right good bowl themselves. And one day
was much like another, except that shortly after
first meeting the abbé news came that Marie
had lost her mother, and many days of mourn-
ing and sorrow passed away.

Once or twice, as they sat in the gloaming

over their embroidery, Sister Gabrielle had
introduced the subject of marriage, and had
mentioned the name of the Comte de Pontorson ; but so withering was the scorn with which
Marie spoke of him that she did not press
it any further. But one day, as they sat at
their mid-day meal, the servant announced the
comte's arrival. Marie, who was sitting next
to Sister Gabrielle, whispered—

" You will not let me meet him alone,
madame ? "

She answered, laughing, " Oh, no ! Ethel and
I will be your seconds, and you shall fire at
twenty paces, an you will."

So after dinner was over they retired to the
private reception-room, where they found the
comte in conversation with Huet; that is to say,
the abbé was showing to his yawning friend
the mechanism of a certain thermometer which
he had had made, and which he insisted on
explaining separately to each member of the
company.

The comte was very polite to Ethel, very
emphatic in his utterances to Marie ; but the
coldness with which she received his choicest
compliments soon reduced him to silence. And
the abbé, who never could see when he was not

wanted, kept coming between them with quasi-scientific remarks, which made Monsieur le Comte draw himself up and stroke the long ringlets of his peruke with a sort of feline softness, looking all the time with eyes that gleamed with contempt and fury. And then Sister Gabrielle, whom the comte always addressed with distinguished courtesy, drew him into the embrasure of the window and engaged him in a long conversation ; and when Huet thought that Marie was listening to his exposition of the proof of revelation, she was all the time glancing at the comte's face, and noting how it grew longer and darker the more the sweet-faced sister spoke, until the angry spot she had so often noticed stood out in all its tell-tale redness in the centre of his forehead. The conference at last broke up by the comte exclaiming—

" I cannot accept the judgment of a nun in such a matter."

" Then why ask it ? "

But the comte deigned no answer, made towards Ethel, and said abruptly, in an undertone—

" There is one way by which your friend can get her father released—for he has been con-

demned to the galleys. Let her accept my hand !
If you, mademoiselle, will persuade her, it shall
be for your interest."

" I thank you, monsieur, for the compliment,"
replied Ethel, haughtily tossing her head.

The comte gazed at her with a look in which
anger gradually melted into admiration. He
audaciously added—

" I admire the devil in you demoiselles
Anglaises. I did not mean to insult you—
indeed, if I were not so poor, I should think
myself lucky to have you for my wife."

" And if you did not get drunk so often I
should be less averse to accepting you," rejoined
Ethel, laughing.

Huet caught the last words, rubbed his
spectacles, ejaculated " Tiens !" and concluded
on the spot that Ethel and the comte were
engaged.

It was agreed that after the comte had joined
them in drinking a bowl of tea they should
all walk on the sands, a thing the two young
ladies had never yet done. But as they were
waiting for the hot water, a servant entered
with a note for the abbé.

" Excuse me, ladies," he said, rising to go.
" I have been ordered by the Parliament at

Rouen to examine a woman under trial for witchcraft, and she waits without."

" Let the poor woman enter," pleaded Sister Gabrielle, " unless monseigneur prefers to judge in private, for I confess I am curious about witches, having never seen one."

The others joined their requests, and Huet commanded the woman to be brought in.

" You have a learned man in your country, mademoiselle," said the abbé to Ethel, " who is almost for disbelieving in the existence of witches. Sir Thomas Browne; I think, is his name."

The comte broke in with—

" And we have a learned man in our country, mademoiselle, who disbelieves in them, but who dare not say so for fear of losing his preferment. The Abbé Huet, I think, is his name."

All laughed at this unexpected sally, and Huet replied—

"We are somewhat smarter than usual to-day ; no doubt la belle Anglaise inspires us !"

The ladies looked at each other and laughed. The abbé thought he had made a point, and laughed too.

But soon the door opened, and an old

crook-backed woman was ushered into the chamber. On her brow was a dark stain of discoloured skin, otherwise she had an ordinary appearance. Huet was about to question her as she stood, but Sister Gabrielle, taking her to a settee, said—

" Here, mother, rest thy aged bones, for thou must be tired."

The sudden change from sullen despair to gratefulness was marked by all.

" God bless thee, lady!" she said with a deep sigh.

" Now, madame," began Huet, in a pompous manner, " I see by these instructions that one charge brought against you is that when a pin is run into that mole you do not flinch ?"

" I shall take care, monsieur, to flinch in future."

This answer was cheered by the comte.

" It gives you no pain ?"

" I can't solidly say it do ; the flesh be most dead."

" Humph! a most unsatisfactory answer!" said Huet.

" I will undertake to run a pin into your finger, monseigneur, and you shall not feel it," said Sister Gabrielle to Huet.

"How! by St. Anthony, not while I have my senses!"

"Oui, oui, merely by tying a string tight round the joint."

"It is true!" broke in the hag, with glistening eyes; "it is true! It stops the blood from flowing, and the blood is life."

"What know you of the flowing of blood, eh?" said Huet sharply.

"More than most, I reckon. Have I not spent my life in learning the duties of a leech; have I not plucked the purple blossoms of the deadly nightshade, and handled the knife, as few others could? Ah! how many a body have I restored to health? What do I know of flowings of blood? ha! ha!" and she let her old croaking voice run its ill-omened gamut.

"Well, if you know so much of plants," cried Huet, "what is in this pot?"

The old woman stooped and put her nose to it, poured some out and tasted it, then clapped her hands. "It is a decoction of the foreign leaf called 'tea.'"

"The devil! I beg pardon—c'est bien curieux! Now, this plant is.entirely new to the country; how came you to know it?" said Huet.

" It is not so new—nothing is new, not even
ignorance. I tasted it years ago, at the château
of the Duc de Mortemar."

" Le Duc de Mortemar ! " cried Sister Gabrielle.

" Parfaitement, madame ; and he had just
such a dimple as you have."

" Oh ! this woman has been chatting with the
servants," cried Huet.

" Let me question her," said Sister Gabrielle.
" You knew Monsieur le Duc, my father ? "

" Oui, madame ; I cured him of a hurt he got
in the Netherlands, and he gave me this little
book."

" Ah ! Charron de la Sagesse ! " exclaimed
Huet, taking hold of the little volume bound
in ivory which the old woman had drawn from
her bosom, and which was suspended round her
neck by a cord of black silk.

" And my father's writing contained within ! "
cried Sister Gabrielle. " What need we further
witness ? "

" I shall send you back to the Parliament, my
good woman, with the strongest expression of
opinion as to your not being possessed—*that*
you may rely on."

" I thank your reverence. We live in an un-

just age, my ladies : *you* can study and get no
mean skill on the clavichord and mandoline;
you can go prancing on your Spanish jennets;
you can write sonnets and madrigals for the
booksellers of St. Jacques, and no man lets or
hinders ye; but an if a poor old woman turn
herbalist to gain an honest livelihood, 'Hey!
there goes a witch!' quoth one; 'Hey! duck
the hag that leagues with the foul fiend!' quoth
another. It's an evil world!"

"Well said for one that hails from the court
of King Petaud!" cried Huet.

"What court may that be?" asked Ethel.

"It is an old saying amongst us, Madame
Ethel, for the beggar class, and derives from
the Latin *peto*."

"It may derive from Latin, or Saracen, but
it lies, anyhow! No man ever saw me beg;
I've noble blood in me, I have, and am related
to princes."

The old hag's claim to noble rank set them
all a-laughing. She was presently sent to the
buttery, and her grievances were smothered
under a weight of good cheer.

But the abbé could not forget the compliment which the Pàrliament at Rouen had done
him in sending so far to consult him, and he

enlarged on the expediency of appointing a
class of savants-ecclesiastic, who should receive
high emoluments and have no duty but that
of thinking and writing. "We should be the
pillars of the Church," he added, glancing
proudly round.

"Or the caterpillars," quietly observed Sister
Gabrielle, as she drew a needle through her
canvas.

"Très bien! Vous avez l'esprit des Mor-
temars," said the abbé, who was always willing
to enjoy a jest, even though it was at his own
expense.

"Mon Dieu!" shouted the comte, who had
sat gazing at Marie with sheepish eyes; "I hear
the fog-bell!"

They all rose and listened. Yes! there
sounded the clang of the warning bell from the
belfry high above, and before the windows
swept a driving mist which hid from them the
distant sea. The next moment one of the
sisters came in to say that the tide was rising,
and a poor man could be seen half a mile away
struggling with the wind and sand. To put on
their masks of velvet and draw their hoods
over their heads was the work of a minute, and
all had presently taken their places with the

excited throng of Montois on the battlements, eager to catch a glimpse of the traveller who risked his life so recklessly, alone on the treacherous sands, when the water was flowing!

CHAPTER V.

THE natives of St. Michel were not the sort of people to look on calmly while a creature, be he man or beast, was lying in peril of his life; and now their brown faces were agitated with something more than excited curiosity, as they shaded their eyes from the wind and tried to pierce the drifting fog. Their acquaintance with danger—for danger and they "were two cubs both littered in one day"—made them not only brave, but modest and serious. The gay selfishness of the Parisian had no reflection in their character; the Montois never boasted of what they could do, never blamed others for their own want of success. The propinquity of the mighty ocean hushed the voice of vain display; the fear of death kept them from thinking too much of this life's joys. Rude, unlettered, totally without regard for appearance,

ignorant of what was happening in the world,
they were, in spite of all that, intelligent, gentle,
happy, and true to the back-bone. Something
they had of English doggedness, something of
German seriousness, and the black eyes and
olive complexions of some of the girls seemed as
though they must have been reared in Spain.

All the time the warning fog-bell was clang-
ing from its wooden belfry, horns were being
blown, voices raised to their highest pitch along
the battlemented walls, and Monsieur le Curé
had numbered the people, which was not
difficult, and found that all were present.
"So it must be a stranger, madame," said an
immense, broad-shouldered fisherman to Ethel,
as they stood together on the ramparts.

Moments of great excitement level social
differences. Ethel and Gustave the fisherman
were talking away like old friends at once.

" Voyez, madame ! If this fog would clear off
he would be safe enough, for there is time to
reach the mound ; all we can do is to stay here
and give him a good shout to show him where
to run. He must e'en be a peddling merchant
from the provinces, to mistake the time of flow
like this ; but, poor boy ! pauvre garçon ! we
must save him if we can."

Between the clash of bells and the blast of horns came to the ears of the listeners a murmur —dull, distant, monotonous.

"What is that?" cried Ethel.

"C'est le bruit de la mer qui monte; in a quarter of an hour we are surrounded."

Ethel shuddered; she began to wonder if the poor traveller had a wife and children at home, who would weep when they heard of his death, or whether he were a young man and the darling son of his mother. The moments seemed like hours; it was impossible not to count the strokes of the fog-bell as it beat out, clang! clang! clang! in a provokingly measured march. How fast she would have made it peal!

Ah! the fog breaks, lifts, vanishes; the sun shines on the rippling surface. Is it water? No; the ripple of the sand but counterfeits the ripple of the wave. Then yet there is time. But where is he? A moment of straining eyes, a cry of horror!

"What?—what is it?" screamed Marie and Ethel together.

But the big fisherman hears them not; he has run to the sally-port, seized a rope and hurried towards a black object rising above the surface of the sand but by three feet or so.

" Assez courageux ! " said a voice behind the ladies.

" Ah, Monsieur le Comte ! has the poor man fallen down ? " cried Marie.

" He struggles in the quicksands, le voilà ! "

" Oh, horrible ! I cannot look ! " said Marie, and covered her eyes with her hands.

But Ethel could look, though her heart beat fiercely and she could count the beatings of her pulse. She watched the figure slowly descending into the sand inch by inch ; she saw the frantic tossing of his arms in the air ; she heard in the great silence which had taken place the fearful cry of the victim, as the engulfing sands sucked him lower and lower ; but she also saw the brave Gustave trailing his rope, and but a few paces now from the sinking man. Suddenly he stops. The ground under his feet makes a noise like the smacking of lips ; he dare not go further. It is a long throw with a double rope ; for as with a lasso he tries to catch him before his head goes under, a long-drawn " Ah ! " from the bastions greets his first attempt. The rope has fallen short ; but a sharply-uttered " Ah ! " and a general movement made Marie uncover her eyes and look. The rope is round him and in his hands ; slowly,

painfully, he is being dragged out. Every eye
was riveted on the two men ; but Marie, who
had not watched the whole, lets her gaze
wander seawards. She catches the comte by
the arm, and screams " Les eaux ! "

Yes! There in the distance glimmered the
rising waters, as they came pouring down old
channels, rushing round banks of sand, cutting
across by river-beds, making huge islands in
their hurry to press forward, clashing madly in
cross-current, and turning white with rage, as if
they were racing to yon hedge of tamarisks for
a wager !

The *curé* looked at his time-piece. " Encore
cinq minutes," he gravely said. Then, waving
his hand, " To your knees ! " And all knelt in
prayer for several seconds. Gustave was to
be seen staggering under the weight of his
burden nearly a quarter of a mile away.

Ethel did not kneel—she could not pray just
then. Once she looked to the brave Gustave,
once to the menacing tide, as if she were
measuring the space and comparing it with
the time ; then she turned impatiently towards
the kneeling throng, as if seeking some one
with whom she could devise a means of escape,
and as she turned, she saw below, within the

walls, some of the dragoons' chargers standing
unsaddled, and fastened to the wall by their
halters. As quick as thought she had un-
fastened two of the horses, mounted one, and
led the other at a trot down the narrow street
and out of the gates.

The clatter fetched every petitioner to his
feet. The dragoons hurrahed; the two horses
pricked up their ears at the familiar battle-cry
and lay themselves out at racing-pace across
the sands. Lieutenant du Hamel capered and
swore and prayed and cried, all in the space of
half a minute, for Ethel had chanced to take
his charger; but none noticed his excitement,
so intense was the interest felt in Ethel, whose
dress floated away behind her, leaving a fair-
shaped limb exposed to their momentary gaze.

Marie was now in a flutter of mingled pride
and fear on her friend's account, and so ear-
nestly did she throw herself into the situation,
that, without knowing it, she clutched the
comte's arm tightly as she leaned forward over
the wall.

"She has dismounted!" was the general cry
of the crowd, whose excited nerves were strung
to their utmost tension. "They have mounted
the stranger behind the Anglaise; now, gallop
for it!"

A burst of laughter.·

"What has happened?" says an old hag, shading her dim eyes.

"See you not, mistress, our Gustave hath slid off t'other side, being but a sorry horse-man."

"That's right, Gus; cling to the mane; embrace him round the neck."

The Montois were French; they could not help seizing the humour of the thing—they would have laughed at Death himself, if he had ·appeared with his cravat awry. Splash, splash! gallop and splash! through the first curdled waters of the flowing sea. They can hear the brave charger panting beneath the walls; only the pool to cross now, and she once more clatters through the gates and up the paved street!

But there is a rush on the walls, people running to the right to see if the charger will go willingly through the deep water. It was above his knees when he started, but many a full wave has deepened it now. See! she pulls him up as he nears it, for she has noticed the different look of the water—not foaming and bubbling, like the shallow waves she has come through, but still and green, and slow-swelling

waves rise and fall upon its bosom. She pats
his shoulder and speaks to him—it is English;
but he puts one ear back. The breathless crowd
above can hear her speak; then, with slow
determined foot, he plods on knee-deep, up to
his girths. Ha! a great swell rising from
behind lifts him from his legs.

"Lean forward!" shout the dragoons.

She has clutched the mane. That last wave
has carried her away from the mount, but the
water grows shallower, and in a moment Du
Hamel and a score of his fellow-soldiers have
surrounded her, lifted her down all dripping,
blushing, laughing!

There was a dark-eyed girl on the walls,
who, when all the rest were looking at Ethel,
kept her gaze fixed on the other horse.
Lisette's olive complexion and oval face had
so won upon Gustave that he had asked her
to be his wife; but Lisette was the prettiest
girl in the town, her father kept the hostel at
the second gate, and all the young gallants that
came to the house fell in love with Lisette.
So she refused Gustave with a pretty toss of
the head, and he never asked her again. But
to-day everybody is cheering the English
demoiselle, and forgetting that it was Gustave

who first dared to venture forth to the quicksands. She is piqued, sorry for poor Gustave,
who is really in some danger, although he can
swim so well. And what business had the
poltroons to laugh when he slipped off t'other
side?. The Montois never back a horse, but
they can swim, and shoot wild fowl, and catch
fish with any one. In short, Lisette was so
indignant with everybody else that she had
a good mind to love Gustave!

And what was he doing? Leaning heavily
on his horse's neck, he comes along, at a trot
which well-nigh shakes his teeth out of his
mouth. Ethel has distanced him by a hundred
yards, for whenever he feels himself slipping,
he jerks sharply at the rein, and so recovers
his balance at the expense of his charger's
temper. At last he reaches the sea-pool, and
all the water is swirling and rushing about his
horse's legs.

"Swim Gustave!" shout the dragoons.

"Swim!" echo the shrill voices of the small
boys, who are anxious to see more fun.

Gustave thinks it safer to trust his native
element and lets himself slide off into the
creamy water, while the charger stands a
moment hesitating, shakes himself like a dog,

and like a dog follows his rider through the deep
sea-pool.   It is fortunate that they are sheltered
from the fury of the tide on this side by the
mount, or it would be hard swimming in such a
mill-stream race as flows by a few yards further
on.   As it is, they are carried landwards almost
fifty yards before they touch bottom, and then
have to stem the current with firmly planted
feet to regain the mound of rock and sand which
rises in front of the gate.

And then the hands that had to be shaken, beginning with Monsieur le Curé and the governor
of the fortress, down to the smallest urchin that
could scream " Bravo, Gus ! " And what a thrill
of pleased surprise when Lisette stepped lightly
out of the crowd of women, and said, with a
bewitching smile, " You deserve a kiss ! " And
how all did cheer, even the most jealous
trooper, when Gustave stooped and laid his briny
moustache upon Lisette's blushing cheek !   Nobody said she was a forward girl, for it was just
the natural thing to do in St. Michel, and was
looked upon as a public attestation of prefer-
ence, which might some day innocently develop
into betrothal, and that into matrimony.

The stranger, who was much exhausted, was
taken into the abbey and placed in a cell by

himself. Being so faint and weak that he was
unable to stand, he was at once put in a warm
bed, and the barber, who shook his wise head
over him, took away a few ounces of blood,
to prevent a fever. During the operation he
managed to get from him that he was an
English seaman, and had been left ashore by
accident ; and this news he imparted with much
gusto to the friars as they sat at supper. Later
in the evening, when he again visited his
patient, he was surprised to find the pulse
weaker ; and, as he could not understand what
the fellow said, he administered an emetic
by way of getting at the root of his uncouth
language, and retired to report progress to the
sister-superior, who was at that time supping
in her private apartments with Marie, Ethel,
and Huet. The comte had taken advantage of
the ebb to ride home.

"Eh bien ! Monsieur le Barbier," said Sister
Gabrielle ; "how fares the unfortunate ? "

"Weaker, madame, weaker; I fear he will
sink. He hath no stamina, to tell truth," and
the surgeon-barber lifted his white apron and
dusted the corner of his eye. It was his *rôle* to
seem to be of a pious and tender disposition in
presence of Huet, whose patronage he wished
to win.

There was a short conference, and finally the barber was ordered to send the wise-woman.

"Now we can try her boasted powers *in corpore vili*," said Huet.

"Do you refer to my nation, monseigneur?" asked Ethel.

"Ah! I forgot at the moment you were Anglaise; you speak our language so perfectly, and we shall soon be addressing you as Madame la Comtesse."

Sister Gabrielle did not seem to see the point of this, but as both Ethel and Marie laughed consumedly, the bishop-elect was well satisfied.

Presently the barber returned with the pretended witch, whom he ushered into the room with every mark of contempt.

Huet addressed her kindly.

"Madame, we have sent for you to visit a poor seaman who lies a-bed sick and weak from his misadventure on the quicksands. Doth your skill go so far as to remedy his hurt?"

The old woman curtseyed low, and replied—

"I can do what I can, but your reverence knows that the issue lies in God's hands."

"Of course, of course; get on, get on!" cried Huet peevishly, taking a pinch of snuff.

"But before I undertake this case, your

reverence, I should like to ask Monsieur le
Barbier here what he hath already done?"

"Certainement! Monsieur le Barbier, explain your treatment."

The barber cleared his throat, smoothed his
hair down, and advanced two steps.

"I was sent by the governor of the fortress
to see the English seaman. The patient lay on
a truckle-bed on his left side. I caused him to
turn over on his right side, as I saw from the
pallor of his face that his heart was affected."

"Or his stomach too empty," muttered the
wise-woman.

"Then feeling that his head was hot and
clammy——"

"From the salt water," interpolated the
witch.

"I prevised a fever, the natural result of his
previous excitement, and I blooded him to
about the extent of five ounces. This had such
good effect that he recovered his senses, from
which I judged that his brain had been con-
gested. A few hours later I found a relapse had
taken place, owing probably to my not having
let blood enough.; and as I noticed a disposition
to kick out his legs, I suspected the presence of
poison and administered an emetic, which hath

worked admirably well—and I wonder what this empirical person could have done better!"

"A nautical surgeon, this! He hath boxed the compass of diseases!" said Huet, with a satirical laugh.

"Cuique in suâ arte," whispered Sister Gabrielle.

"Now go and see the sick man, madame, and bring us word what you would do; but on your life try no remedies until they have been approved."

In less than ten minutes the twain returned.

"Well, madame?" said Huet.

"Humph! might be better," said the hag.

"What! Hath not the emetic worked?"

"The surgeon-barber is a wiseacre, that I will not deny, your reverence.' |

"Softly! don't malign the minister of Æsculapius."

"I don't comprehend fine lingo like that. I go by mother-wit and keeping my eyes open. I say that blockhead hath done more harm to his patient than good. He found him weak, and he let him blood and made him weaker; he found him starved for want of food, and he gives him an emetic—to bring up the lining of his stomach, I suppose! A pretty minister of

Scalpius, forsooth! You might scratch his scalp
with a boat-hook and find ne'er an ounce of
brains."

"And how would you treat the man, my
little wise old woman; dic nostra Sibylla!"

"I would command the *chef de cuisine* to
make him a *potage;* I would fetch from the bin
a bottle of seasoned Madeira wine—I dare say
the old abbots of St. Michel have laid some
in store. I would keep him warm in bed, and
wait till he made some fresh blood to replace
what yon parrot-headed chirurgeon threw
away."

"Ma foi! an original physician! So you dare
contradict the faculty, Sibylla nostra, and maintain blood-letting to be apo skopou, minime ad
rem."

"I am no scholar, your reverence. I generally find one word enough for one idea; and if
I must be curtailed, let it be of fine words
rather than wise thoughts."

"Ha! the Sibyl on education! Then it seems
the labour I and my coadjutors have spent in
editing the classics, 'in usum Delphini,' has
been wasted!"

"You speak hard things for an old woman
rightly to come by, and may-be your reverence

is mocking an old ignorant body that never had
no schooling. What them there class-books
were I can't say; but if they were mainly poor
worthless thoughts dressed up in a suit of brave
words, I should say your reverence *had* wasted
your time. A man liveth not long, and he
needs learn just what is useful for this world
and the next, or he cumbers himself to no
purpose."

"La! how the Sibyl doth moralize, Sister
Gabrielle."

"Methinks, monseigneur, the poor old
woman gets hard treatment from you; for
my part, I confess I shall lay to heart what
she hath so courageously said—amicus Plato,
sed magis amica Veritas!"

"Eh bien! nous verrons! Go, Sibylla, and
ply thy *potage;* to-morrow we will see thee
again on this matter."

When Ethel and Marie retired to bed that
evening they discussed the events of the day.

"I would I were as brave as thou, ma chère
amie," said Marie, throwing her arms about
Ethel's neck.

"I would I had as constant a lover as
thou!" rejoined Ethel, pinching the other's arm
playfully.

"Nay, thou hast won the heart of Du
Hamel," answered Marie, taking her remark
seriously. "A boy-lover, truly, is better than
none! You should have seen him weep and
dance for joy when the bay charger set you
dripping in the gateway."

"But Monsieur l'Abbé means me to wed
Monsieur le Comte, Marie!"

"Ha, ha! No wonder he makes such mis-
takes; he is always turning everything into
Latin verse. Mais, dites-moi, what think you of
this English seaman? Comes he not with a
message from Lieutenant Henri?"

"Ah! probably yes! Shall I not contrive to
get speech with him to-morrow?"

So talking they fell asleep; and when the
new-born sun was dancing on the wave, a light
tap on the shoulder awoke Marie, and as
she opened her sleepy eyes, Sister Gabrielle
said—

"Get up, my sluggards! you talk too long
o'nights. I came to tell you, Marie, that a friend
of yours has come in the night to stay with us
a while. 'Aunt Justine,' she bids me style her,
so rise at once to join us at *déjeûner*."

"Why, auntie, what brings you here?" was
Marie's exclamation, as she kissed a tall, prim-

looking old lady, in a very high cap of plain muslin.

"My religion, my dear," was the stern answer, accompanied by a fixed and stony stare. "Yes, my religion—I thank God for *that*, at all events." (An uncompromising look at Huet, who was buttering himself a hot roll.) "Yes, my dear, your dear mother and I—now don't cry, for goodness' sake don't, or I am unmanned!— what was I saying? To be sure! your poor mother and I have both suffered at the hands of the Jesuits. I shall refrain from characterizing that body with any epithets. It is better to pass by with silent contempt the brutal outrages of which that most heartless, unchristian, and, I *will* say, diabolical society have been guilty. But I level at them not a single word of censure. May God in His infinite pity find some room for pardoning them, if indeed He can find it consistent with His un-swerving justice to do so." Aunt Justine uttered the last words in a tone not to be over-looked, even by an Infinite Being!

"Pray, madame, control your excited feelings," cried Huet, with a mouth full of fish.

"Monsieur! comment! et pourquoi! Have you, sir, no pity for a broken reed, bowed to earth by the waters of affliction, thrown beneath the wheels of your priestly Juggernaut, and deprived of that poor solace, even, a change of linen ?"

Monsieur l'Abbé got a fish-bone in his throat, which developed itself into a violent fit of laughter ; the company in general suffered from fish-bones. Aunt Justine shot fiery glances round, and now addressed herself to Ethel.

" You, ma chère, are a Protestant, and I feel I can look for sympathy in you, though, to be sure, you never had a stick of furniture to lose for the sake of your faith. But that matters not, they will find some other way to make you suffer, I shouldn't wonder. Thank you, madame," [to Sister Gabrielle] "you have helped me plentifully. You know what a pretty villa I had—how neat the lawn, the garden, how choice my pictures and tapestry. Well, my dear, all gone! furniture smashed! myself very indecently treated !—though, for my religion, I could suffer worse things without complaining— and what for ? what for ? I repeat."

" For attempting to sell your property and quit the realm," replied Huet quietly.

" You astonish me, monsieur, you perfectly

astonish me! It is true I *was* about to reside
abroad for a space of years, chiefly on account
of the unpleasantness arising from the king's
mistress—well! just one glass more, madame,
it is so· very luscious—where was I? Oh!
with the king and his mistress, of course! I
was about to winter in a foreign country, where,
of course, my little villa would have been out of
place, so I instructed my agent to dispose of it
for me, when one night, as I lie abed, I hear
trumpets on the front lawn and drums amongst
the asparagus, and before I could put anything
over my night-dress they had beaten down the
door and entered my bed-chamber! Mon
Dieu! the horror of that moment! Some of the
gay young cavaliers pressed round me to shake
hands, others rushed up to embrace me; but I
called upon God, and He sustained me with a
constant severity of countenance which effec-
tually repulsed the most brazen. And then,
hélas! they broke up my pretty wardrobe—
inlaid, you know, with cedar—spoilt my dainty
curtains, threw out of window my valuable
antique china, rifled all my desks and cup-
boards, and next day sent me on a sumpter-
mule to join you. Such are *my* sufferings! But
you must understand I do not complain; and

if it has pleased God to afflict with unusual severity one of His elect, as I hope I feel myself to be, no doubt it is wisely ordained—thank you, madame, I could not possibly eat any more—and perhaps I may be the means of converting some poor benighted Papist from the error of his or her way." Aunt Justine smiled a sickly smile across the table, and bowed to the company on either side of her; then, catching sight of a beautiful little cabinet which stood on the sideboard, she cried, " Ah ! that is just the exact counterpact of the Japan cabinet which the dragoons broke up, les monstres ! "

" Then permit me to have the pleasure of offering it for your acceptance, madame," said Sister Gabrielle, who had all along used much tact in pacifying the infuriated martyr.

" You forget, Madame l'Abbesse, that I have no roof to cover my head."

" Pardon me, if I seemed to forget your unfortunate position ; but it is not so bad as you imagine, for the Holy Church will always give you a home either here or in any religious house you may prefer."

" I thank you personally, madame, with all my heart. If I might be allowed to quote from

a book which I believe the 'Holy Church'
thinks lightly of, you 'are not far from the
kingdom of God.' But as to my showing any
gratitude to your Church for robbing me of my
pretty, pretty villa" (here Aunt Justine shed a
tear), "and insolently offering me a lodging in a
convent in lieu of it, it is out of the question."

When Marie and Ethel were left alone that
morning with Aunt Justine, they found her
much softened, and she would often drop her
knitting and burst into tears. The memory of
her happy home, where she sang the Psalms of
David with such trust in the protection of God,
whom she served, according to her lights, with
her whole heart, contrasted so bitterly with the
tiny cell on the dreary, sea-girt rock, that at
first, in the flush of bitterness she was ready to
upbraid Providence for allowing the wicked to
triumph over His elect. It needed time to heal
the fever of the hurt ; there was a world of
religious pride and stubborn will to beat down,
ere Aunt Justine could kiss the rod and profit
by the chastisement that the God who loved
her permitted.

In the afternoon, as it was too stormy to walk
on the rampart, the abbé invited them all to
drink tea, and showed them his astronomical

and meteorological instruments, all of which Aunt Justine looked upon with suspicion, and was with difficulty prevailed upon to look through a microscope, because, as she severely asserted, " if the Almighty had wished us to pry so narrowly into the secrets of nature, He would have fashioned our eyes accordingly." To which Huet replied that he was surprised not to see her nude and without clothing, because, if the Almighty had wished that she should wear clothes, He would have fitted her accordingly— an argument which so tickled a boy who was at that moment pouring hot water into the tea-pot that he burst into a loud guffaw ; but this so incensed Aunt Justine that she boxed his ears soundly, saying—

" I'll teach you to sit in the seat of the scornful ! for shame, you misproud boy ! "

However, some confectionery which accom-panied the tea restored her to good-humour, and they sat till it grew dusk and the sea came swirling and plashing once more about the granite walls.

" I think we shall have a fine night; my barometer rises," said Huet.

Aunt Justine was just in the mood to save a soul pleasantly, and she asked with her blandest smile whether barometers were ever made use of by the good men spoken of in the Bible, and if not, whether it were not presumptuous in a child of Adam to try and falsify the Word of God, which saith, " The wind bloweth where it listeth, and thou canst not tell whence it cometh and whither it goeth."

" Yet even the hypocrites of those days, madame, could discern the face of the sky."

" It is perhaps hopeless to think that you and I can agree ; but I do wish, Monsieur l'Abbé, that you would not try to go beyond the Word of God, which contains all we need know, and every word, every letter—aye, every dot and iota—of which is infallibly true."

" Is that a chronometer, madame, I see suspended to your girdle ? Fie, fie ! one who loves her Bible should, methinks, carry about her the sun-dial of Ahaz!"

Aunt Justine murmured something about the Devil quoting Scripture to serve his ends, but her remark was lost in the tones of a clavichord which Sister Gabrielle began to play.

And the vaulted chamber was filled with the melody of sweet sounds. The three voices blending together in the vesper hymn, the silent stars that rose and twinkled through the casement,

the distant sighing of the restless ocean—all
tended to soothe the wounded spirit; and whilst
Huet mentally composed an Alcaic ode to the
music of the spheres, Aunt Justine prayed and
wept and was comforted.

CHAPTER VI.

ETHEL and Marie were again in their own little room, plying the needle and discoursing on the events that had caused them such sorrow, when the door of the apartment creaked on its hinges, and peering between the candles they saw the face of the wise-woman in the open doorway.

" Entrez, madame."

She came in, leaning on her stick and panting with the exertion of having mounted so many steps. " If Madame l'Anglaise is not too busy, would she come and speak to the English sailor ? He is now much recovered, but speaks such vile gibberish it makes a woman's ear ache to listen to it."

Ethel hesitated. Would Marie accompany her ?—must they ask leave of Sister Gabrielle ?

" Oui, oui ! it is the lady abbess who suggests the visit. I shall be there too," says the old woman.

Whereupon the two girls descend to the dormitory in which the seaman now lies. It is a long low chamber, with two rows of beds along the walls, down the centre of which they must pass to reach the last pallet on which the sick man is stretched; a feeble light burns above his head, which leaves his features in gloom. The witch sits down at some little distance ; Marie gives Ethel a push, " Do not be shy—I follow."

Ethel crept on tip-toe to the bed-side. It was too dark for her to see if he were asleep or no. She paused a few moments before speaking, and then said—

" We have come to see how you are, my friend."

" I am bettèr," with a stress on the last syllable.

Ethel turned at once to Marie and whispered, " That is no English accent ! "

The sick man half-raised his head, and put his fingers on his lips and pointed to the old woman.

" What do you want ? "

" Make to go out the nurse; I wish you tell something," in a voice half-spoken, half-whispered.

As the two girls hesitated, he put out his

hand and touched Marie on the arm. She started, and thought she heard him pronounce her name; she stooped, and he whispered again—

"Marie, Marie! c'est moi, Henri."

A thrill passed through Marie's frame. Her heart fluttered. She would have sunk to the ground had not a chair been there for her to fall into. Was this like acting up to her first great resolve to think no more of him as a lover? True, she had let herself think of him in the long absence, when she fancied no harm could ensue to her; she had talked with Ethel about him; toyed with the golden memories of the past, and deemed it no wrong to build impossible castles in the air. But then, they were such pageants of the air—they seemed so fantastic, so unreal. What harm could there be in indulging the imagination, so long as her mind, her imperious will, was fixed on having no converse with an atheist. Yet now, when she saw him lying on the sick-bed, tended by stranger hands, all the bloom of her first girlish love returned to grace this, her riper fruit. Her heart yearned towards the dark-eyed boy, whose liquid eyes and dimpled cheek were still so fresh in her memory. She leaned over him and stroked the

stray curls off his brow, and he, looking up
into the heaven of his hopes, murmured "Ma
petite!"

But the witch had been watching and listening, and came suddenly to the bed-side with—

"Morbleu! The English seaman, methinks,
is an apt scholar and a hasty wooer. Comment! What! learned the tongue and won the
maid in a trice!"

Henri turned to her and said—"Hush, grandmère! your tongue shall be tied with silver and
weighted with gold. These demoiselles and I
are old friends; and hark ye, when you thought
I slept you prayed aloud, goody, and I heard
you. You are no Catholic, but a Huguenot,
like myself, and you cannot betray me."

"Betray you, sweetheart? Non! I would as
soon betray my first-born! Now I have your
confidence I will help you, sweet ladies. · There
be not so much love in the world that it will
bear marring and thwarting. Now let the doves
coo together, and you and I, mademoiselle, will
linger by the door." And she was beckoning
Ethel to follow her, but Marie said—

"I must not stay here alone; Ethel, do you
remain and talk to Henri. Lovers, forsooth!
you silly old woman, old friends, I tell you."

And when the two girls had smoothed his sheets and shaken up his pillow, they asked him to tell them how he came to cross the sands towards St. Michel. "But not if you feel too ill to tell us," added Marie. And Ethel set the candle so that the light fell upon the face of the sick man, and in a moment they both exclaimed together, with gestures of surprise.

"What is it?" cried Henri.

They had braced up their nerves to see a shrunken anatomy of manhood, hollow cheeks and sallow, and behold! the light fell upon a rich, manly brown, the Henri of old, only maturer. The same light danced in his dark eyes, only with less of wild fire and more kindly; the same dimple nestled on his sun-kissed cheek, only the smoothness of youth was fringed with the silken curtain of manhood.

"What is it?" he repeated.

Ethel made answer. "We are surprised to see you looking so strong and hale. Are you really ill?"

Henri laughed.

"Who is the sceptic now, I wonder? eh! Marie? Nay, in good sooth, yon old woman can tell you I was exhausted yesterday, for I had tasted bit nor sup for many hours, and the

struggle on the sands with death had given
me 'le dernier coup'; but, thank God! I have
a good constitution, and I am as well as ever,
since the goody there gave me the food I
craved.   To say I was an English sailor, and
to lie tossing on this hard pallet, all this was
but a ruse to get speech with thee and Ethel,
if I may address her so, since we are all old
friends together."

"And do you indeed thank God for His
mercies?" asked Marie, with a trembling voice.

"Indeed, I do so, with a heart from which
man's cruelties have smitten away all its pride.
Ah, Marie! to suffer much is to feel and believe
much.   Reason has long since got beyond her
depth, and is fain to lie in the bosom of faith."

As Henri dropped his brown hand heavily
on the counterpane, a little white hand timorously fluttered to it, like a bird seeking her
woodland nest.   It was Marie's!

"But I must narrate to you both what has
happened to me these few days.   First, let me
tell you Philippe is safe." ("Deo gratias," from
Marie.)   "And now, to go back to that dreadful
night — the night of the attempted flight — I
waited till morning broke with my six-oared
galley on the beach, listening for the sound

of wheels, but nothing was audible but the
monotonous roar of the surf. I ran—it must
have been a dozen times—to the top of the cliff,
to see, if possible, the flicker of your links ; but
nothing met my eye but the row of tall poplars,
which seemed to bow their heads with sarcastic
politeness in the moonlight, and bow me down
to the beach again. Ah ! how my heart beat
when a stronger gust of wind than usual
brought mysterious sounds floating to my ears.
The neighing of a horse from· some distant
field, the whirr of a bat's wing—so that they
have wings—put me in a fever of expectation ;
and so hour after hour passed, and no coach
appeared, no horseman rode up with tidings
of your coming, and at last, with a heavy heart,
I was forced to put back to the frigate, carrying
with me a few of the country-people who were
of 'the Religion.'

"When I stepped on deck, poor old Maintenon looked me full in the face with such a
sad, inquiring glance, he quite smote my heart.
The sailors said he had been restlessly running
fore and aft all day, stopping sometimes to lift
his foolish head and howl. I could not help
thinking of a passage in your great play-writer,
Ethel, which my father taught me to read,

where Jacques moralizes over a wounded stag—
' the hairy fool,' as he calls it ; and so thought
I—' Poor fool, with your wistful gaze, I cannot
bring you your master nor your mistress, but
we will try and find them, for all that.'   But
the next day I saw the patrols riding along the
coast, and the day after that, too ; so we set sail
and coasted along about twenty miles, and there
Maintenon and I landed, and made our way on
foot to Coutances.   I took care not to enter the
town, but one day I spent in the ivy which, you
know, covers the ruined span of the ancient
aqueduct ; then, while it was night, made my
way to Pierre's lodge.   It was deserted, and I
walked on to Guillebert's farm, with my hand
on my friend's collar, since he was for making
straight for the château.   Eh ! ma foi ! poor
Guillebert came out to me, his eyes streaming
with tears, told me the sieur had been con-
demned to the galleys, that you two had been
taken hither, and, worst of all, that madame
your mother had been tormented to death."

   " Oh, non, Henri, say not that ! tell me she
died in childbed ! " cried Marie.

   " Ma chère, I can only tell you the truth !
Your sainted mother died a martyr's death.
They kept her baby from her till it was too late

for both, and two souls fled to Heaven together
—the mother's and the son's.   Oh ! how devilish I felt when that honest fellow recited to
me her sufferings !   The cowardly Benedictine
prompted it all, for the Jesuit had disappeared.
Some day I hope to call the monk to account,
and won't I shrive him with a leaden bullet !
These inhuman cruelties make one's blood run
cold ; a religion which prompts such diabolical
outrages seems to me the worship of Satan ;
and I will never make a friend of one who puts
his trust in the Pope of Rome ! "

As the young man spoke he withdrew his
hand violently, and the little white fingers were
left alone.   Marie thought of another night,
when a hand was as suddenly withdrawn from
a protecting arm.   But then it was she who
severed the links of love ; now the cruel
wrench had come from him !   And she sat pale
and proud, with the tear-drops for her mother
frozen on her long eye-lashes, and all the
torrent of her feelings arrested, pent up by
those hasty words.   But as he went on to speak
of her home, she could not but listen.

" Honest Guillebert sheltered me in his house
that night and the next day, too.   I wanted to
have a look at the old home before I went

away, but dared not go by day-light, for a mob
were at work, stealing and destroying all they
could lay hands on ; and in the afternoon of
that day, Guillebert came running in to tell me
that they had fired the château ! And there, in
good sooth, was the smoke curling upwards
over the dark pine forest in which we have so
often hunted, Marie. At midnight Guillebert
accompanied me—though I begged him not,
for he ran great risks if he were caught with
so rank a heretic—and we three, to wit, the
farmer and I and Maintenon, set out to walk
through the woods towards the château. It was
a quiet, moonlit night, and many an old clump
of trees I marked standing on the familiar
sandy knoll as we passed on to the kennels.
Eh bien! when we arrive there, we see such
ruin and disorder ! Doors off their hinges, the
stables littered with dirt and straw—and you
remember how neat they used to be, and how I
used to love watching the stable-boys plaiting
the straw twists that bordered each stall!—and
now all was desolate and dreary. We were
moving away, when I missed Maintenon. I
gave a low whistle, and he answered me with
a whimper.

"'Mon Dieu!' said I, 'he has found some-

thing!' and I ran back to see what it was;
and there, to be sure, I found him licking something that lay upon the ground.

"I stooped—faugh! what a sight met my
eyes! There lay drenched in gore poor old
Richelieu, the oldest hound in the pack, and
many years the fleetest. Le pauvre chien! as he
lay on his side, his tongue out, his eyes blood-
shot, methinks he recognized my voice, for he
just flapped his tail once on the ground, and
twitched his ears back—aye 'tis a dog's welcome! I know it well—and it moved me sorely
that I could do the old hound no service; yet
'tis something when you lie wounded unto
death to feel the gentle touch of a hand you
know, and Richelieu seemed to appreciate our
sympathy. Nay, Ethel, I do not wonder that
you weep; I myself felt the tears rise as far as
my throat, but I choked them down.

"'Come, Maintenon,' said I, 'we must leave
the poor fellow!'

"And much ado had I to draw him away;
he was for ever trotting back to give his old
playmate a last lick. 'Truly,' thought I, 'in
the love of the brutes must be reflected the
mind of God! Deus est animus brutorum,' as
your dear father used to say; and Richelieu

was no heretic—what did the fiends want to
shoot him for?

" But I must on, or they will come and disturb us. We entered the grounds of the
château at the foot of the hill, passed through
the park, where so many wet-nosed Jersey cows
used to feed—but no dappled darlings trampled
the dewy grass now; on through the tourney-
ground and past the maze, from which the
ensign staff had been rudely plucked; past the
marble basin where the Triton of brass, that
used to cast his girandola of water thirty feet
high, was trickling ruefully enough; and up the
green slope to the terraces, when we saw the
façade of the building grimed with smoke, the
roof fallen in, the windows wrecked, the two
towers that flank the wings, being of thicker
masonry, still entire; but such a dismal show
I never wish to see again! But the moon shone
on that once fair château and showed us her
windowless frame, like a skull with eyeless
sockets, while wreaths of smoke hovered about
her turrets, like a dead man's hair blown about
by the wind; and all the lawn was strewn with
garbage and fragments of dainty equipage,
ruined bronzes and gnarled bones of mutton
and goat lying cheek by jowl!

" Long time we stumbled about, not caring much to enter the château, whose doors stood wide open, lest a burning rafter should come down on our heads ; and, indeed, the stone stair-case had cracked and parted with the heat, and there was nought to see within. And Maintenon —he stole close at my heels with his tail down between his legs—I never saw so abject a creature. I could feel his muzzle close to my leg at every step. Enfin, we think of leaving, for there seems little profit in squandering our time amongst these ruins ; yet we stood for a moment by the white tower under the cedars, casting one silent look at the old spot. Guille-bert refrained from speaking, for he saw my heart was too full for utterance ; and, indeed, I was standing with my head upon my breast, plunged in a mournful reverie, when Maintenon suddenly startled us by leaping up, with a suc-cession of short barks, and running to the postern in the white tower, which was still closed.

" ' Ciel ! there is something there ! ' cried Guillebert ; and we both ran to the postern.

" There was the hound, his nose close to the ground, sniffing loudly at the bottom of the door, and now and then wagging his tail, as

'twere to encourage his nose, and then looking up in our faces with the same sharp, joyous
bark, the which we would have checked, since
it might have led to our discovery; but the
mastiff grew so excited, now sniffing, now barking, and now running round the tower, as if
seeking some place of entrance, that we were
sure there was some treasure-trove worth our
grappling.

" Eh bien! We looked well about, but there
was no window by which we could enter, and
the door looked too strong to batter down in
an hour or two. Fortunately, a cedar-tree grew
very near the tower, and up this I climbed, till
I was on a level with a narrow lancet window;
but still a distance of several feet prevented
me from looking within. However, a branch
grew out towards the wall just above the
window, and I found, as I climbed on to this,
that bending with my weight it brought me on
a level with it. All this was done so quietly
that not even the birds which roosted in the
branches awoke from their sleep! And now
I thrust my head in at the window, but see
nothing, on account of the gloom; yet I seem
to hear a step approaching on the stone staircase. It comes to the chamber apparently, and

a shrill voice is raised, 'Au secours!' I could see nothing, but the voice seemed familiar. I shouted through the window—you must know the walls were immensely thick—'Qui va là?' and what was my joy and surprise to hear, 'Ah, Henri! est-ce vous? me voici, Philippe!'

"Was he not half-famished? you ask. Oh, no! fortunately a store of provisions, biscuits, and water had been laid up. But they were glad to get out! Who, do you say? I forgot to tell you that Father Beretti was found in the chamber above. Well, to make a long story short, we got them out by Beretti's window, which he had contrived to enlarge; but without me they could not have touched the cedar branch, and with my help, I promise you his reverence clomb down the tree but awkwardly! I made Beretti give me his word of honour not to escape, and we all set out for the farm."

"Henri!" exclaimed Marie, "thou art a kind and brave friend. May God reward thee!"

The icicles had long ago thawed from her eyes and melted in the summer rains of gratitude. He might now refuse to love her, but she felt for one moment that she could not help loving him; the next, she knew she was wrong, and prayed, "Sancta Maria, ora pro nobis."

Henri looked at her changing countenance and was silent.

" And where is Philippe ? " asked Ethel.

" The next night we set off for the coast, where I had ordered the galley to be waiting, and Beretti and Philippe and Maintenon accompanied me on board the frigate. But we wanted to hear news of you, for we knew not whether you had been carried elsewhere or no, and so I disguised myself as a common sea man, and set out along shore for St. Michel, which I should have reached just before the flow, had not some officers of the patrol caused me to make a long circuit in order to avoid their observation ; and when I saw the tide coming in, 1 was obliged to risk falling into the quicksands, though I know the coast hereabouts as well as any man. And now I fear lest some of the Montois shall recognize my face. My plan had been to hide in Gustave's cottage—not a Montois would betray me ; but Ethel's grand rescue lodged me in the jaws of the lion, whence it will task my wits to get forth. How if we all escape together ? "

" Bien dangereux ! " murmured Marie ; and Ethel added, " For if we fail, our lot will be far worse then it is at present."

"Yet, Marie, there are dangers here from which I would you were removed."

"What mean you, Henri?"

"I mean that the Comte de Pontorson is no safe neighbour for you."

"What! is he not a man of honour! He dare not come at me by violence, and certes, he shall not by persuasion."

Henri looked admiringly on the flushed cheek and glancing eye, and muttered—

"Cependant, mon amie, I wish you were free of him."

"And why so, monsieur?"

"Because he hath designs upon you. In plain, words he would marry you."

"And if he would, what is that to thee, with thy new-found heresy?" And Marie, struggling to keep down the swelling tear and to master her trembling voice, was yet fain to fling herself with the semblance of haughtiness out of the dormitory.

"What have I said, Mistress Ethel?" asked Henri in consternation, when the last flutter of Marie's habit had disappeared in the doorway.

"Nay, I know not that you said aught that a maid should not willingly hear—unless it were," she added, "that some time ago you swore a Papist should never be your friend."

"Curse my folly!" muttered Henri.

The convent bell began to toll, and Ethel escaped through the low doorway, and Henri was left sick at heart.

CHAPTER VII.

THE street of St. Michel was deserted, though
it was scarce ten of the clock, for the Montois
retire to roost at an early hour. There was
no sound of festive revelling in the *cabaret*, because nobody in the town had any money to
spend in drink. A happy sobriety, the result
of an empty pocket! The sentinel on the walls
leaned heavily upon the masonry, and fell a
dreaming of cakes and cider. The cat that
crept under the shadow of the tiny church
seemed to think it superfluous to call for his
mate, since he was the only cat in the parish.
Walking down the unevenly paved street a man
would see no sign of wakefulness. Nobody
stole the wet shirts of flannel that were hung
on ropes across the street from window to
window, because it was not worth a thief's
while to come to so meagre a city. Two or three

Benedictines had set lights in their cells ; and
the charitable, if they looked up at the grim
abbey, said " The friars, holy men ! are at their
prayers." Usually, the only man who kept
awake after ten o'clock, except the sentinels,
was Monsieur l'Abbé d'Aulnay, and the vulgar
put it down to the "hay-water," as they styled
his Chinese decoction, which they would not
have tasted for anything !

But to-night there was an exceptional
debauch in the second hostelry as you enter
the town. Lisette's father had invited a few
boon companions to celebrate Gustave's exploit,
and Gustave had been allured to his feet, on
which members he had made a brief oration
that did more honour to his heart than his
head. However, the company had now dis-
persed, and Gustave lingered a bit to help
Lisette put away the pewters and straighten
the chairs ; and as Lisette's father flung himself
into an arm-chair—a rare piece of furniture in
St. Michel—and seemed inclined to chat, Lisette
set two chairs by the still glowing hearth, for
the nights were cold ; and what so natural as
that the lovers should settle themselves there
side by side, talking so confoundedly low that
Lisette's father first angrily demanded each sen-

tence a second time, then assented with a grunt
to every remark that was made, and finally
drivelled into a nodding unconsciousness!

And there they sat, not saying much to one
another, for ideas did not flow so fast as salt
water at St. Michel, but quietly enjoying the
situation. For to Gustave it was a sort of
essence of bliss to peruse the warm, oval face,
to dive fathom deep into the liquid eye, to feel
the touch of the shapely brown hand, to
admire the well-turned foot and ankle—bare,
like the legs of all Montois, men and women,
as often as they could get rid of the cumbrous
sabot; and Lisette was well pleased to be
admired by the strong, the brave 'swimmer,
who had saved so many lives by his prowess;
and if she sighed, it was that her mother lay
in the rock-bound churchyard, and she has
none to advise her, shall she marry Gustave
or wait? And she let her thoughts run on,
slipping swiftly to an unknown future. Some
happy scene, to be sure, she pictured, for a
sunny smile was lighting up her olive features.
Rudely broken was the chain of thoughts, when
the latch was suddenly lifted with a sharp click,
and a woman's face, closely veiled, appeared in
the door-way.

"Holà!" shouted the old man, half-awake.

"Eh quoi, madame!" cried Lisette, just turning in time to recognize one of the nuns from the convent.

"Pardon! I seek Gustave, and am told he is here. Ah!" she exclaimed, as, entering the dusky kitchen, she saw the object of her search.

Gustave had risen on hearing himself named. The stranger unveiled, and the fisherman's face relaxed into a welcome grin. "Bien! c'est Madame l'Anglaise!"

Ethel, looking first at Gustave and then at Lisette, said—

"I want to speak a few words in private to you, mon ami, if you will permit me."

"Oh, Lisette and her father are just the same as myself—no secrets—all true, mademoiselle; speak out, and never fear the old man will blab. I'll answer for Lisette, here."

So Ethel was compelled to sit down and unravel her private skein of thought.

"The seaman whom we saved from the quicksands is no seaman after all, but——"

"Oui, madame," broke in Lisette; "we know who he is well enough—Monsieur Henri Guillot, son of the old captain who used to live up at Avranches. Gustave knew him."

"Bien! If you know him, that makes my
task easier. You know him well perhaps? have
fished with him? would be glad to do him a
service?"

"Aye! Many's the time we have fared forth
together, fusil on shoulder, in the dead of the
night, carrying a lanthorn and seeing the sea-
birds stare us foolishly in the face. He's a
bonny, brave garçon, and help him I will, an
he want it."

"Thank you, Gustave! He does want your
aid now. You know, of course, that he is of
'the Religion,' and is sought for by the king's
officers. Well! you and I, he says, have placed
him in the abbey, and you and I must get him
out."

Gustave grinned, showing a row of teeth
somewhat worse for wear. Lisette pulled his
moustache and said, in her coquettish manner—

"Allez! release the lieutenant and I will
reward you with some little trifle. Une affaire
d'amour peut-être." The last words were said
aside, but Ethel overheard them.

"You are mistaken, Lisette; Monsieur Henri
is a friend of Mademoiselle de Cornelli and her
father—not of mine."

"Ah! c'est égal! il y a d'amour quelque part.

Young ladies do not travel abroad at night unless the business is urgent."

"So, Lisette," answered Ethel, "you think love is a woman's sole business. Monsieur Henri has saved the life of Monsieur Philippe de Cornelli, and that alone is enough to make me run a hazard for him. I would run a hazard for Gustave, because he has shown himself a man of no ordinary worth."

" Then madame thinks Gustave good enough to ask Lisette's hand ? " said the girl, with a pretty toss of the head.

" I know not, Lisette, what your wit and temper may be; that you have a pretty face I can see. But I think of the Spanish proverb, 'A pretty shoe makes a bad slipper.' What I say is, that she is a very lucky girl who gets Gustave to wed her ! "

Poor Lisette, the spoilt beauty of the community, hung her head and pouted. She had not drawn breath in so bracing an atmosphere since she first stole out of childhood. It took her a few minutes to get over this moral slap on the back ; being before so high in her own esteem, she seemed to herself to have sunk to degrading depths. But Ethel turned to the embarrassed fisherman, and said—

"Do you think we can possibly get him out of the abbey to-night? Every hour is important, you know."

Gustave stood, poising a profound chin upon a thoughtful forefinger, and at last answered, in deliberate tone—

"Oui, certainement, il se peut."

"How?" cried Ethel.

"By the tramway for provisions, voyez! Run and tell the lieutenant to be ready in an hour's time at the great wheel. He will show you where it is, for he knows the abbey well. I shall be at the bottom of the tramway, and Lisette—Lisette, ma petite!—will you come and help, too?"

"If madame thinks me worthy," said Lisette, in humble voice.

Ethel squeezed her hand silently.

"Bien! Then you shall pull up Lisette, and she will help you to let down the lieutenant, who is too heavy for you alone; the great wheel might fly round too quick, voyez-vous? Then you can let down Lisette easily, and I will show monsieur how to get over the walls. Bon! the tide will be at ebb."

Ethel uttered a few hasty words of thanks and hurried back to the abbey. The frère let

her in, suspecting nothing, as she was often
visiting sick folk at all hours, and the Bishop
of Coutances had written asking that their
detention might be made as easy as possible.
First, she went to Marie and acquainted her
with the scheme, then she sought the wise-
woman and bade her tell Henri to seize some
pretence for leaving his chamber, and she then
got a cassock and chapeau as a disguise. She
then returned to Marie to wait for the time
appointed.

"You will come, Marie, to the great wheel,
for we want help?"

"I would rather not; but if I must, then
must I."

"You have misunderstood Henri, ma chère.
He never thought of you when he spoke so
fiercely about Papists."

"Perhaps so, Ethel; but I have considered
the matter well, not without prayer, and I am
sure, moi aussi, I ought not to wed a heretic!
Surely my own unhappy family is a proof of
the evil of conflicting religions in a household."

"In France, I grant you; mais, ma chère,
suppose you both come to England."

"The warfare would be none the less between heart and heart. I know Henri. He is

not gentle and many-sided, like my dear father, but hath an impetuous way of thinking and feeling, which brooks no contradiction. I must either break with my husband or my faith; I feel it, Ethel."

"I am sorry, Marie, very sorry, for your sake and for his. I would not have you act against your convictions, but I would you could talk with one of our Anglican divines, when I feel confident you would be persuaded that we are a Catholic Church, holding the Catholic faith ; and perhaps in the bosom of our Church you and Henri might be united in heart and soul alike."

"Ma foi, Ethel! what sayest thou? The Anglican a Catholic Church! Why, the fat wife-beater made heretics of you all—rank heretics! Nay! but if King James should, in God's mercy, draw the realm back to the true fold, then perhaps—— "

At this moment the door opened, and Henri appeared in his disguise as a priest.

"Eh! Father, you have mistaken your chamber!" exclaimed Marie, not recognizing him in the gloom of the apartment.

"Then, madame, am I well disguised!" rejoined Henri, laughing.

Then passed a few hurried words of farewell. Ethel was to apprise Gustave of any change that might be made in their place of detention, and Henri was to endeavour to find out where the sieur had been conveyed. All were to live in hope of soon freeing themselves and taking refuge in Holland or England. Hope is no laggard in the breast of youth, and he mightily upbore their spirits to-night.

They soon, however, saw that it was time to make for the great wheel, *la grande roue*, by which provisions were carried up to the abbey on a sort of tramway constructed almost perpendicularly up the face of the rock. The wall, called *la Merveille*, is boldly planted on a conical pedestal of rocks, piled *pêle-mêle*, like the ruins of a gigantic land-slip. The slope of the clift descends so rapidly to the sea that it forms itself a colossal wall, monstrously carved and sculptured by chance. Below, the rocks bury themselves in the sand. On the top of this natural wall a thick and solid mass of masonry, built with glacis to meet the irregularities of the rock, supports a construction of incredible magnitude, which shoots from a single stem, as it were, to burst out in tower and turret two hundred feet from its first spring, and which

looks out on the sea by every kind of opening,
majestic or elegant, denticulated with a fretting
as fine as lace-work or the honeysuckle that
climbs the window of a country house. It was
on this side that the tramway had been constructed, to save the trouble of carrying provisions up the convent steps. A large wheel at
the top wound or unwound a rope to which
was attached a pannier, and this ascended or
descended the shallow groove which had been
cut in the face of the cliff.

But it was no such easy matter to thread the
labyrinth of passages, vaults, staircases, cloisters,
and guard-rooms which lay in the way of the
three adventurers before they could come to the
platform ; for they did not dare use a torch, lest
they should attract attention. They marched
in single file, Henri first, and already the clock
had struck eleven when they stumbled out of
the shadows of the *salle des gardes* into the
starlight. How sweet was the air, blowing
from distant orchards and thymy hills! The
white houses of the little town of Avranches
were faint in the distance ; the murmur of the
far-off tide seemed like music in a dream! Short,
however, was the time for enjoying Nature's
charms. The rope was already vibrating—the

signal that was to warn them when Lisette should be ready to ascend. So they grasped the handles of the wheel, and swiftly drew in the rope, till at last a head appeared above the black rock, and a lithe figure sprang on to the platform. Henri took her hand.

" I wish I could give thee some reward for thy trouble, fair Lisette ; but I must be thy debtor till better days."

The girl drew herself up proudly as she answered—

" Lisette takes no payment for helping a friend. Should you give me money, I would fling it yonder."

" Lisette hath gained two more friends ˙to-night," whispered Marie, as she, too, pressed the girl's hand.

Henri placed himself in the crate, and the girls took their places at the wheel, and the last they saw of him was his priest's hat waving in the air for a last adieu ! Again the rope was shaken ; he had reached the bottom. A second time the rope was drawn in, and now Lisette was lowered.

But there was one officer in the garrison that night who had not gone to bed. Lieutenant du Hamel had been composing sonnets to his

lady's eye-brow after the fashion ridiculed by
Molière, and then sat gazing at the stars, his
elbows resting on the window-sill. Having
worked himself into a pretty frenzy of abstrac-
tion, he arranged his flowing peruke and
sauntered out upon the battlements, passing the
sentinel, who saluted him, without any recognition, insomuch that he, with the superstition of
a Breton, spat thrice upon the ground, believing
that he had seen an apparition. But the eyes of
Du Hamel were fixed upon a certain window,
behind which slept the paragon of her sex,
thought he; and as he stood with his back to
the bastion, wishing he had the wings of a bird,
hoping chance would give him some way of
manifesting his devotion—aye, 'twould be easy
to die for such as she—his eye caught sight of
figures standing on the platform—figures of
women; and one tall—none so tall as she in
Mont St. Michel, save mademoiselle. Oh, horrible sight! the figure of a man stands beside
her. Then some lover pays her nocturnal visits
when *he* is asleep! Ha, ha! this shall be his
last.

With such dire thoughts Du Hamel returns
for his sword, which he buckles truculently to
his side, and runs, not this time round by the

walls, but more directly down the rough and stony street, to the ledge of rocks on which the tramway rests its lower extremity. Just as he emerges on the ledge, having had to climb a few feet up a narrow gulley leading from the street, he spies a muffled figure stepping from the crate and shaking the rope to signal those above. To stride across the intervening space and tap the intruder on the shoulder was the work of a moment; then, striking a fighting attitude, he shouted—

" Draw! I challenge thee for the fair lady up yonder! Draw, I say!"

" Draw what?" said the cloaked stranger, in a soft but startled voice.

" Now, by St. George, thou shalt not hoodwink me, thou cuckoo, thou night owl! draw thy craven sword, an thou hast one!" and he made a pass in the air.

" Peace, peace! Monsieur l'Officier, you know me not. I am only Lisette, daughter of the old man who keeps the second hostelry as you enter the town."

" Le Diable!"

" I pray you do me no hurt; I have supped with the young lady."

" You have?" cried Du Hamel, whose love

had soon conquered the chagrin caused by his ridiculous mistake. " You have supped with her ? Tell me, did she speak of a certain officer in the Guards, the Royal Horse-guards ? Did she not prefer a red uniform ? Did she seem to carry a paper of some fifteen sonnets long concealed in the bosom of her dress ? "

" She did, monsieur ; and I marked she spelt them over constantly."

" Attendez, ma petite fille ; here is a gold coin for thee ! So she was moved somewhat, vous croyez ? she had an air distrait ? she did not answer you straightway ?"

" Non, monsieur ; she is in love, *sans doute*, but with whom I may not guess."

" Attendez, ma chère ; here is a small piece for the trouble I have further put thee to. Not a word now to any of the garrison, and I am thy true friend."

The gallant fire-eater strode back to his lodging a happier and more hopeful man. The mischievous girl ran as fast as her bare feet would carry her, longing to tell the tale to all the gossips, and see how they shouted with laughter.

Meanwhile Gustave had shown Henri a way to descend the walls by St. Aubert's Spring, the

sacred waters of which had first leapt forth at
the bidding of the holy bishop who founded and
built the abbey. For a moment he stood on the
parapet watching the retreating figure till it was
lost in the shades of night. The sentinel
approached Gustave and winked, shrugged his
shoulders, poked him in the ribs.

" A boon companion, eh ? "

" No, a love affair," whispered Gustave; " best
say nothing about it, mon camarade."

" Bon ! you shall owe me a flagon of canary
for this. Bon soir ! "

The business of the evening had thus
finished successfully ; everybody was pleased.

The next morning great was the surprise to
find that the seaman had fled. The surgeon-
barber was examined, the wise-woman was
examined, but the only conclusion was that the
English are a wild, insular race, that bear not
confinement, and, like wild animals lured against
their will, take the first occasion of escaping,
without utterance of thanks. Huet was especially learned and diffuse on the subject, and put
Ethel to the blush by quoting from passages
in Sir Walter Raleigh she had never read.
However, both the young ladies were glad that
the abbé's geographical lecture had precluded

the possibility of putting awkward questions concerning last night's escapade.

Déjeûner being over, Huet was sitting, as was his wont, for half an hour in Sister Gabrielle's saloon, listening to a *chanson* from Marie; Du Hamel and Ethel standing by an open window which gave upon the sea, to-day blue and sparkling, as it played about the mount for a few minutes before retiring to the distant low-water mark. Du Hamel was radiant with happiness as he entered the room. The pretty-featured Lisette after all had been his only rival; but he stood in a strange perplexity when he heard that an English sailor—*the* English sailor—had escaped in the night. The harpsichord and the *chansonette* covered his confusion. Ethel was leaning against the open window; he resolved to try conclusions with her.

" 'Twas a beautiful night was last evening, was it not, madame ? "

Ethel started a little and bowed her head.

" The stars were so wondrous bright that even objects at a distance were mightily visible."

Ethel turned her large blue eyes inquiringly upon him. The young officer coloured like

a girl, and could say no more for full five
minutes. When he found words, the superior
tone of banter had been stolen from him; with
a desperate effort he blurted out the words—

" I saw you on the platform ! "

"Saw whom ? " asked Ethel in a feigned
surprise.

" I think I had the honour of observing your
figure in the star-light; I could not mistake it."
Then, exchanging his courtly tone for one intended to carry a grave rebuke, " And the man
whom you helped to escape was the Englishman—a gallant disguised as a seaman. Fie !
fie ! "

Ethel could scarcely resist laughing, the poor
young man looked so comically distressed ; but
she rejoined, with an effort to meet the occasion
with becoming dignity—

" If you were not so excessively young, Monsieur du Hamel, I should consider what you
have said just now an insult ; but I put down to
ignorance the indiscretion of which you are
guilty. Perhaps you think that the fact of my
being so poor and unprotected warrants you in
addressing me as you would address no other
lady. The Englishman to whom you refer in
such coarse terms, though almost a stranger to

me, and certainly for whom I entertain no such
unworthy feelings as you suggest, would, I
doubt not, be willing to measure swords with,
you in defence of my honour!"

Tears of repentance were streaming down
the smooth cheeks of the love-sick officer. He
would have grovelled on both his knees, he
would have trampled on his periwig in contempt of himself, if she had bidden him.

"Oh! I have done you a wrong! I lay the
humblest apology that a French officer can
make, low at thy feet. Say! can I hope to be
forgiven before I die?"

Ethel gave him her hand with one of her
frank smiles.

"Go, Sir Lieutenant, and say no more of this
to any one, and some day I may tell you my
secret."

Du Hamel kissed her hand, retiring with the
fragments of the cup of joy which had been
dashed from his lips, partially cemented.

In the middle of the day, when Marie and
Ethel were passing the door of the monks'
refectory, a familiar voice sounded in their
hearing.

"By our Lady! I told you so, sir; I told you
we should do better to lodge at the clergy-

house in Avranches, where all things are fairly
and wholesomely administered. See, Monsieur
le Jésuite, what comes of posting hither on a
Friday, of all days in the week! Here we are,
eight persons at dinner, all told, and what does
the cook put before us but a poor par-boiled
Jean-doré? Monsieur, I told you how we
should fare!"

"Listen!" whispered Marie. "That is the
voice of Father Beauvais!"

"And those sound like his sentiments," said
Ethel.

After dinner Father Beauvais came with
Beretti into the *salon*.

"Why, father, what brings you here?"

"A retreat, my sister."

"A retreat!" cried Marie. "Have you then
tasked your energies over much?"

"Hush! I bring you a letter from monsieur
votre père," whispered Beauvais.

"Ah!"

Beretti approached, looking pale and sad, a
great contrast to the red-faced, kind-hearted
glutton by his side. He took both Marie's
hands in his, and looking into her face with a
strange tenderness, said—

"Daughter, we have both suffered. You

have lost a kind mother, and I a beloved
sister."

Marie wept.   He drew her to the window.

"Oh, if I had been free, this would never have
happened ! The Benedictine might well fly after
killing that sweet saint.   Alas, alas ! sorrow for
you, for me, for all who knew her, for Holy
Church !   But *requiescat in pace !* You have
heard, perhaps, how I was rescued from the
dungeon in the white tower ? Oui, Monsieur
Henri treated me very well. We have agreed
that for my freedom I am to use my influence
to set monsieur your father free, and for that
purpose I go to Paris shortly."

" God grant you success ! " murmured Marie,
wiping her eyes.

Beauvais returned.

" I must repeat what I have just been telling
Sister Gabrielle. The Jesuits with their extreme measures are ruining the Church — all
head and no heart makes a very bad man, say
I.   I have witnessed cruelties enough the last
month to ruin a good stomach, let alone the
Church."

Beretti looked darkly, and answered—

" Peace, with thy witticisms at this moment !
There has been a gross mistake, I agree with

you ; but a hardened sinner can only be met by hard measures. In such cases, if the Holy Church were to be guided by the sentimental maunderings of such as Father Beauvais, heresy would be rampant. Aye! ye think my heart does not bleed for the poor silly sheep! God knows every blow that falls on a heretic falls on Father Beretti!"

CHAPTER VIII.

MARIE retired to her own chamber with her father's letter, and, locking the door, sat on the bed with folded hands, hardly daring to break the seal and read its contents, which she knew must be so sad. But when, bending her head over the silver crucifix which hung about her neck, she had murmured her prayer to Him who was acquainted with grief, she pushed back the brown hair from her forehead, and unwound the silken thread by which the letter was tied. It was written in the form of a diary.

"To my beloved daughter I have sent these lines by the hand of our trusty chaplain, Father Beauvais. Carried from my home by dragoons, my dear wife lying a-bed with her infant—God speed them both! Rode a horse which shook me much; legs tied beneath his belly, though

I gave my parole not to attempt escape.
The people at St. Lô flocked about us, many
pressing my hand with their lips; women weeping, which did much anger the dragoons, who
struck about with their flat swords at the poor
folk. Lodged in a noisome prison at Caen,
where I have so often fared sumptuously; none
of my old friends ventured to visit me. Sick
at heart and willing to die, but wondrously
cheered by an aged prisoner who did admonish
me to trust in Jesus; listened to an account of
His sufferings, and felt ashamed to complain
more.

"A wearisome journey to Rouen, where, as we
entered the city, I saw some regiments of the
cuirassiers and Royal Etrangers, commanded
by Choiseul Beaupré, riding sword in hand.
Conducted first to the town-hall, where Monsieur le Marquis de Beuvron wept to see me
in so sorry a plight, but was compelled to
order me to a dungeon; here my clothes were
searched, and all my money removed by the
turnkey. Next morning brought before the
governor and interrogated; convicted of
having intended to escape from the kingdom
against the ordinances of the king, and sentenced by the court to be taken to his majesty's

galleys, and to remain there in penal servitude for life, with confiscation of property, etc. A relief to hear my sentence, and to feel that I am suffering for the truth. Oh, that my dear children may have strength to bear their own sufferings, and to bear witness that I have done what is right !

"Obliged to eat sour bread with my water, and to lie on the stone floor, as that rascal stole everything, to the last pistole. The *curé* came to see me, asking me if I were not a-weary of my hardships, and urging me to renounce my errors ; who, when I ventured to argue with him, cut me short, and entered upon so wearisome a discourse that I did not deign to listen. Received a visit from the Archbishop of Rouen ; assured me of his love and sympathy, that it was entirely by the king's orders I was confined and punished.

"'Then who persuades the king ?' quoth I. 'Do not the Jesuits and the Bossuets ?'

"The old man shook his head sadly. I was as sorry for him as he for me. I told him how all my pistoles had been stolen ; to my comfort they have been returned, and I can buy soup and wine' occasionally. Another batch of Huguenots came in this morning. I was amused by the ignorance of one of the chaplains who was sent to convert them.

"'I have come,' saith he, 'to convert you to the Christian religion.'

"'Mais, monsieur,' say they, 'we are Christians, both by baptism and by our faith in the gospel of Jesus Christ.'

"'What!' says he, 'you are Christians? Repeat to me, if you please, the articles of your faith.'

"'Very willingly,' said they, and began to repeat the Apostles' Creed.

"'What!' cries he, 'you believe that!'

"'Aye!' say they.

"'And I, too,' quoth he, shutting up his tablets, on which he had writ their names. 'Monseigneur l'Évêque hath been making a fool of me! I had always heard that Huguenots believed in nothing, and were monsters of iniquity. I ask your pardon, gentlemen'; and so the simple-minded old man quitted the prison.

"Saw a chain depart for Havre de Grace; all who were to start mustered in the courtyard, chained by the neck in couples, with a thick chain three feet long, in the middle of which is a round ring. Then all placed in file,

couple behind couple, et puis, a long and thick
chain passed through all these rings, so that all
were chained together, about four hundred in
all, who sat down on the ground until the
Procureur-Général of the Parliament came to
give them in charge to the captain of the chain,
and so to the galleys.   There is some talk of
my being sent to Paris, as all the galleys here
are full.   Father Beauvais has visited me,
telling me of my dear wife's murder, and the
poor child's.   Cannot write on such a subject.
What is this life worth now ?   How I long to
meet my beloved where persecution is not !
God's will be done !"

Marie let the letter drop upon the floor, and
burst into a flood of tears.   It seemed to her so
cruel to punish the gentle, forgiving father,
whose influence for good had been so marked
over all with whom he came in contact.   And
the poignancy of her grief was increased by the
fact that it was upheld by the Holy Church of
which she was so faithful a member.   The
saints and angels of her imaginings had assumed
the guise of fiends ; her moral nature had received a shock ; she almost said to herself,
" There is no God ! all religions are falsehoods
and man's conceit ; the world is a dungeon ; why

await the executioner? Let me die! let me
die!"

So, sobbing and rebelling against her early
teaching, she fell into a slumber and slept for
some hours; and, little by little, sleep that knits
up the ravelled sleeve of care, calmed the
emotions of her troubled heart, though now and
again some heavy sigh would swell her bosom
as she slept, as on a dull day the long wave of
yesternight's commotion swells upon the bosom
of the placid sea. And when she awoke, it was
to find Sister Gabrielle kneeling at her side,
watching her with the tenderness of a mother,
as Marie's eyes opened with that questioning
wonder of the recent voyager to dreamland.

Sister Gabrielle stroked the brown tresses
back from her white brow, and drew her finger
lightly along the pencilled line of eyebrow, as
if to efface the lines of care which might be
gathering on Marie's young face.

"Thou hast slept, my child, and I trust thy
heart has been set on Him who alone can heal
its wounds," said the abbess.

Marie sighed; to awake was to return to the
world of heart-aches, to the life of disappoint-
ments, of cruel clashings between duty and
desire.

" Monsieur le Comte has ridden over, bringing you some beautiful grapes, ma chère."

" I thank him, mother; and yet I would he
had not brought them. You know my feelings
towards that man; I cannot love, I will not
wed him."

" God forbid that I should press thee against
thy will. Father Beretti had hopes that thou
wouldst be an instrument in God's hands to
draw him closer to the Holy Jesus; 'twere a
noble work!"

Marie flushed as she replied hastily—

"Father Beretti is for sacrificing all that
makes life joyous on the bare chance of doing a
good work. I know not if the good God be so
exacting as some of His priests are; but, an He
be, then am I a black sheep indeed, for I will
not wed that man, not if the saving of his soul
hang on the answer, yea or nay."

" Hush, my poor child!" said the abbess,
embracing Marie.

" Instead of converting him from his evil
ways, I should be dragged down with my
husband. Alas! I am but a weak girl; my mind
takes its colour from the people with whom I
live, and that makes me wish, dear lady abbess,
to enter a religious house and to profess the

life of a nun. Do take me back with thee to
Fontevraud !"

"Non, ma chère, it is too soon to decide so
momentous a question. And if thou wilt reflect
a little with me, thou wilt see that thy wish to
become a sister is not altogether a right one.
For just now thou art beaten down and bruised;
the future looks dark to thy human eye, thou
hast nought to set thy heart upon, and thou
offerest to bring thyself as the bride of Christ!
It is as though one should offer a gift which was
worn out; it is to make the religious life a
dernier ressort. 'Tis often done, I fear, but 'tis
not piety."

Marie hid her face in her hands and sobbed.
The abbess let her cry in silence for some
minutes before she added—

"Monsieur le Comte prayed me to give thee
a message from him. I have reserved it till I
heard you express your feelings towards him, as
his communication lacks the tact of a lover, to
my thinking. I was to tell thee, Marie, that the
king will allow thee to keep thy father's estates
if thou marry the Comte; otherwise the brother
of Madame de Maintenon is for buying them
for himself, and thou wilt be left penniless!"

Marie looked up with a light sparkling in her
eyes.

"C'est bon, çà ! God has found a sacrifice for me at last! Why, before I knew that, I could not help feeling that I was preferring my own pleasure in refusing his hand. But now—Oh! my good lady, thou hast made my heart right with God. I give up all my lands that I may not wed with a libertine!"

"But not that thou mayst wed a Huguenot! Ah! thou dost start at my words! I have had thy story from le père Jésuite. Ah, Marie!"

"Madame, you do me wrong. I have resolved never to marry Henri Guillot, whom I know not if I love or no. We were children together, played in one garden, rode the same pony. His father was my father's friend; and we are much beholden to Henri, too. But I have seen the evil of wedding with one of an alien faith. If it be a sin so to wed, surely we have paid the full penalty. Madame, I promise thee never to marry one whose faith shall conflict with mine! Henri, too, has said as much for himself. And now, madame, take me to Fontevraud!"

The lady abbess folded the girl to her bosom, and an hour went by whilst they communed together. When at last they returned to the *salon*, they found Huet and the others at the window, looking through a telescope, all talking together, and the tea nearly cold.

" I will swear by the glass—it is one of Huyghens' make," cried Huet.

" What is toward, my friends ? " asked Sister Gabrielle.

" Regardez, donc ! " and Huet offered her the telescope.

The sea was now surging round the rock, the back-wash meeting the coming wave and forming a circlet of watery pinnacles around the mount, which sometimes jerked themselves into a sheet of spray ; about half a mile away a black object was moving on the water. Sister Gabrielle dropped the glass.

" It is some live animal swimming towards us ! "

CHAPTER IX.

LIFE at Mont St. Michel was not so headlong
but that the appearance of a strange object on
the sea could evoke a certain measure of excitement. The news spread like wildfire amongst
the pious friars, and from them to the lay
brethren who helped in the menial offices of
the monastery ; and the lay brethren promptly
pointed out the novel intruder to the soldiers
on garrison duty, and the soldiers chatted with
the fisherman's pretty bare-legged daughters,
and in about five minutes all the inhabitants of
the town who were not bedridden had clustered
together on the ramparts, making a Babel of
confused voices, where nobody listened to
everybody's chatter.

As usual, Du Hamel had by mere accident
found himself close to Ethel and Marie, who,
with the rest, had hurried out to see the sport.

The lieutenant was loading his piece, in case the creature should come near enough to be shot. Every kind of conjecture was being hazarded on all sides. It was a whale, it was a porpoise, it was a drowned man floating, it was the devil out of his proper element; but whatever it was, there was no doubt that it was drawing nearer and nearer. As it rose on the top of each long wave it presented itself a good mark for the sportsman, though the rapidly falling shadows somewhat blurred its outline. Du Hamel raised his carbine.

"Do not shoot, monsieur; is it not a dog?" exclaimed Ethel, grasping the young officer by the arm.

"Oui, oui!" cried several voices; "le chien! le voilà!" And a general stampede ensued along the walls, as the dog seemed to be making for the entrance. They could hear him panting now, and sometimes the glint of the white of his eye was visible, as from time to time he half turned his head to take his whereabouts. Like a flock of school-children the Montois ran down the stone steps and towards the gates, to see the dog that came from no man's land.

As Ethel walked quickly after them, with Marie, she whispered—

"Mon Dieu! did you not observe?"

"Observe whom?" asked Marie.

"Maintenon!" replied Ethel.

They hurried on, saying no more, for the presence of Maintenon suggested many surmises. When they reached the second gate they saw the mastiff casting about with tail erect and nose on ground, moving alternately right and left, until he stopped in front of the hostel which was kept by Lisette's father; there, as the door was shut, he halted, and lifting his head in the air, barked loud and peremptorily, as one who was not in the habit of being kept long waiting.

"His master is there!" whispered Ethel.

"How dost thou know?"

"Comment? Does not Maintenon say so, as plain as may be?"

"Alas! the dog, then, will betray him," said Marie sadly.

"Perhaps it would be wiser for us to stand aloof, for if he recognize us, we shall at once be associated with the person in the hostel, whoever he may be."

Marie assented, and they turned to depart. They had not got many steps before Du Hamel overtook them.

"So the mysterious animal turned out to be a big mastiff, mesdames, belonging, they say, to a sailor who came ashore this morning."

"Vraiment!" said Marie, assuming as natural a tone of interest as she could.

"I have to thank you, mademoiselle, for preventing me from killing him."

"Oui, monsieur; it is easy to take away a life. I always marvel how it is that you men are so fond of destroying innocent creatures; it seems to me, if you will pardon me, a childish cruelty."

The lieutenant bit his lip.

"When shall I learn to please mademoiselle? I am for ever being taunted with my boyish folly. Diable! I will try and perform some action which a man should do." So saying, he swept the ground with his long feather and quitted the ladies in high dudgeon.

After supper, when Marie and Ethel sat in their chamber plying the needle, a servant announced Lisette. The pretty brunette entered with a graceful bend of the head, in which there was no acknowledgment of inferiority, for the Montois, men and women, know nothing of artificial aristocracy. As soon as she was seated, she stated her errand. Monsieur Guillot was in

her father's house, and wished to see the ladies
to-night. But Marie refused to go, and en-
treated Ethel to accompany Lisette to the
hostel. On the way thither Lisette was loud
in her praises of the young sailor, declaring
that she loved him next to Gustave, and
wondered how Marie could refuse to see him.

"But it would not be proper for a young
French lady of noble birth to visit a gentleman
secretly by night," said Ethel.

Lisette pondered a while, and then remarked,
in a soft interrogation—

"Mais, mademoiselle, do the demoiselles
Anglaises, then, visit their lovers as we are
doing ?"

"Hush, Lisette! we are on no lover's errand,
as you must know; besides, the hunted rat does
not curtsey to her pursuer."

They found Henri with Maintenon lying by
his side, his black nose as near the blazing log
as he dare lay it. The dog, as Henri explained, had been brought with the sailors in
the boat from which Henri had landed the
night before, but had probably refused to
return to the ship without his master, and had
leapt into the sea whilst the galley was being
rowed back. Ethel was startled to hear that

Henri and Philippe were about to visit Rouen,
to get speech with the sieur, if possible; and
she told him in return what Marie had learnt
in her father's letter, that it was probable he
might be taken to Paris.

"Ah! that is important news!" cried Henri.

"It may give you a clue, monsieur."

"Monsieur?" said Henri, a little reproach-
fully; "nay, an I be not something nearer than
that, dangers knit true friends in vain."

"Eh bien, mon ami! some day I may call
you Henri, if the troublesome burrs of theology
can be swept clear."

"I understand!" said Henri; and then, lower-
ing his voice, added, "You will, I am sure, help
me in my suit, and clear me of all false suspicions in my Marie's eyes."

Ethel had risen to quit the hostelry, and was
standing with her hand on the handle of the
door, which was half open; Lisette, who had
been peeling apples with one ear open to the
conversation, also rose to accompany her.
Ethel smiled at the sailor lover, and giving him
her hand said—

"Soyez heureux! and may we meet again
under better auspices!"

Henri, still holding the girl's hand, stooped

and kissed it reverently, and at that moment a cloaked figure passed the door a few paces off.

"Allons, Lisette! we must hurry home," said Ethel, and they set off up the lonely dark street.

Arrived at the convent, Ethel narrated to Marie what she had heard.

"And does he leave St. Michel to-night, Ethel?" asked Marie.

"Oui, ma chère, under cover of the darkness he goes to Tombelaine, whence, at the morning's flow, the galley comes to fetch him."

A short pause ensued, then Marie said—

"I have a head-ache; let us put on our velvet masks and sally forth on the ramparts. There the air is fresh and wholesome—stay! here comes Aunt Justine! Oh! chère tante, wilt thou walk with us on the walls a while?"

"What, now, child? God forbid that I should be guilty of conduct so light and unbecoming a maid! 'Twould give the enemy an occasion of slandering."

The Abbé Huet put his head in just then, muttering "Justine, deterrima belli causa," when Marie begged him to accompany them without in such piteous sort, that he was constrained to

consent to her prayer; and then Aunt Justine felt
it her duty to go, too, in spite of the garrison
and the lumbago.

It was a still, clear night in early November.
The moon was riding in the blue sky and behind occasional clouds of fleecy gray, through
which the infinite azure was seen like veins
running through white marble. In the distance
sounded on this side the lapping of the far-off
sea; on that, the tinkle of the sheep-bell amid
the sparse clover and the lumps of peat; but
one not familiar with the phenomena of St.
Michel would have thought that the moon-lit
ripple which stretched away from the sandy
banks of the Coesnon was the surface of the
many-dimpled ocean, instead of what it was, a
trick of the delusive sands. And the shadow
which lay black athwart them might have
seemed the body of some gigantic monster,
lying sullen, with folded wings, under the lee of
the ponderous rock. The aspect of the place
set the gazers thinking, silent, each listening to
the tones of the strings upon which the magician
Nature was playing. Æschylus had written
words that went with the music of the soul to
which Huet was enthralled, David had sung the
shadow of a great rock for Aunt Justine's medi-

tating, to Ethel the floor of heaven was thick
inlaid with *patines* of bright gold, and Marie's
soul was communing with her mother's, the
latest saint she had added to her calendar.
And thus they strolled round the battlemented
walls, now stopping to lean over the breast-
work, now startled from their reverie by the
whirr of a bat, or the hooting of an owl.

When they had walked almost to the Well
of St. Aubert, and Huet was discussing the
velocity of sound to half-bewildered ears, and
Aunt Justine was reflecting on the nature of
extremes to meet, as exemplified in the case of
a superstitious Church begetting an atheistic
spirit of philosophizing beyond the Written
Word Marie suddenly broke in with an exclamation of surprise—

" Ecoutez donc! what noise is that below ? "

The rest stopped to listen. A faint sound as
of clashing swords seemed to come from below
the walls. They leaned over and looked down ;
a mass of large boulders piled one on another
prevented them from seeing what was going on,
but the hack, hack, of swords was unmistakable,
broken now and then by short pauses, in which
the crunching of pebbles seemed to argue the
combatants shifting ground for another assault

at arms; and again the heavy hack, or the grating whistle of the subtly turned steel, almost setting one's teeth on edge, was renewed with fresh vigour.

For several moments the party on the wall remained speechless; there was a kind of spell in the rhythmic swish and hack of the steel which prevented them from giving the alarm. Aunt Justine was the first to break away from the enthralling interest of the contest, and away she sped towards the sentry, who was dozing at an angle of the wall. But before she could return with him the clash of swords had ceased; a low moan came sailing on the frosty air, and a dark figure in the distance was striding rapidly towards Tombelaine. The sentry levelled his musket and fired; but the powder flashed in the pan, and he invoked his saints in vain. Presently he cried, as he gazed along the sands—

" Sapristi! 'tis not to be marvelled at that my musket missed fire. See, mesdames, how a little imp that lay squat yonder waiting for him, now leaps and bounds with infernal delight by his side!"

" It is true!" said Aunt Justine; "it were useless to waste powder on him "

"Aye, it would ask a silver bullet to pierce his fiend's skin. I knew we should have trouble when that witch was loosed amongst us."

"Oui, oui," replied Aunt Justine; "you went against revelation, Monsieur l'Abbé, when you presumed to pronounce so rashly on devilish possession."

"I did not presume to deny the existence of witchcraft, madame, though one Reginald Scot hath a century ago urged some plausible reasons for disposing of that belief; yet, on the other hand, the learned Casaubon expressed his faith in them, and your own King James the First, with somewhat of over-pedantry, mademoiselle."

"Pardon, monseigneur! but while we dispute of witchcraft, perchance some poor fellow may be dying below there for want of aid," said Ethel.

"Peut-être!" replied the abbé, and ordered the sentry to climb down and see.

He did so, and soon shouted back, "It is an officer, well-nigh killed!"

Aunt Justine hurried back to the convent to apprise the chirurgeon, and the others hurried out through the gate, opened by a drowsy sentinel, and round the outside wall until they

came to the spot where the soldier was supporting the body of the wounded officer.
Blood was flowing from his head, and his pale
cheek was envermeiled by a crimson stream
which ran sluggishly on to his lace cravat,
dying it the colour of his *justaucorps;* his
perruke lay on the rocks, beside his jewelled
sword.

"Who is it?" cried Marie and Ethel in a
breath.

"It is the poor Lieutenant du Hamel," said
the dragoon.

Then, in a moment, Ethel remembered how
a figure had brushed past her as she bade
adieu to Henri in the hostelry. The poor boy
had doubtless followed his supposed rival, challenged him to a combat, and fallen a victim to
misplaced jealousy!

They carried him carefully to the convent,
Ethel helping to support his head; and as she
looked upon his wan face, made all the more
ghastly by the flaring of the torches, she could
not help accusing herself of having driven the
young man into this sad adventure by her
taunts; and the eyes that so seldom were wet
with tears had dropt two or three very large
specimens of the same before she recollected

herself. But they were shed entirely out of
pity, and not the least from any affection to
the wounded boy, as she kept mentally observing, so soon as she was again sufficiently
mistress of herself to analyze her own emotions.

But when she and Marie lay down side by
side in the convent bed, there arose a stout
argument between them as to which of the two
duellists was in the wrong; and, considering
that neither of the disputants knew anything
about the cause of the fight except what they
could conjecture, it was not to be wondered at
that the last syllogism was not concluded when
sleep overtook them, which it did not before
they had kissed and made friends. So Marie
fell asleep with a smile on her lips, following in
her dreams the triumphant Henri; but Ethel
tossed on the bed of care, filled with some pre-
sentiment of coming trouble. But she did not
know what part of her horizon the cloud would
darken.

CHAPTER X.

THE Sieur de Cornelli was not suffered to remain long on the rotten straw of his dungeon, after his agent in Coutances was able to send him some money. The gaoler was amenable to pistoles, and soon found for his prisoner a more commodious apartment, where for two or three weeks existence was made tolerable by a copy of Montaigne's "Essays" and the visits of sympathizing friends. But one morning the governor of the prison entered, rubbing his hands with quiet satisfaction, and said to the sieur—

"We have got a vacancy for you at last, monsieur!"

De Cornelli looked up from his papers with a gleam of hope in his eyes.

"What! where?" he sharply demanded.

"At St. Malo, near your old home, in the galley *La Favorite.*"

De Cornelli felt crushed for the moment, but quickly recovering himself, inquired when he was to start.

"To-morrow, s'il vous plaît. You will find everything in capital order ; the captain of the galley is an old friend of mine, and will treat you handsomely."

The sieur at once wrote to his agent to instruct him where to remit money, and to Marie to acquaint her of the change of plan. As for money, it had dwindled down to a modest sum held by the sieur's agent as the realized value of a small estate which had been sold before the troubles began. The rents of his estate were now paid into the Treasury, and Madame de Maintenon had advised her brother to buy the land as soon as it was in the market. But De Cornelli tried to console himself with the thought that his sacrifice would bear fruit in time to come, and if he and his children were beggared of this world's wealth, it was that others might reap a harvest of spiritual welfare. Yet when the moment of suffering had to be faced, he felt sorely tempted to confess with Montaigne that mankind were not worth the sacrifice, that it was better, like that garrulous champion of amiable selfishness, to throw overboard honest convictions and enjoy life. He was tempted; but immediately the devil left him in disgust, as being one on whom he could not palm off the riches of this world in exchange for the answer of a good conscience towards God.

It was a weary trudge to St. Malo, over muddy roads and bleak plains, and through the rude *bocage* of Lower Normandy, where no creature met the eye save some poor peasant woman, looking more like a wild animal than a human being in her shaggy goat-skin, which kept her uncouthly warm. The miserable shanties that were dotted about the neglected fields sent forth few loud-voiced children, now that Louis the Grand, the Magnificent, had made France athirst for glory. For their fathers had long ago bit the dust in the van of a victorious army; and the children's soup grew daily more and more *maigre*, and the little ones chirruped with more and more of plaintive yearning, until the great King on the white horse stooped down and kissed their faded eyes ; and Rachel refused to be comforted, for women do not understand how glorious it is to shed blood in a noble, wholesale manner !

"La gloire, c'est une bêtise," said an old

crone to the captain of the chain, as they rested at Pontorson. She had lost father, husband, and three sons in the king's wars, and might claim to have earned a right to criticize the march of events; but for all that the brutal officer struck her on the mouth for her want of patriotism, and made the blood flow.

"Shame on you, coward!" said a voice from among the convicts, to the consternation of all; and chains clanked and rattled in an uneasy wonder.

"Who said that?" demanded the officer of the archers who guarded the chain.

"I did," said the Sieur de Cornelli, in a firm voice.

"Très bien, mon ami," replied the man, "we shall look to your morals presently."

That night all the convicts were ordered to range themselves on one side of the inn-yard and strip off all their clothes. Having done this, they were to march naked to the other side, and remain there till the officers had examined their pockets. It was a bitter November night, and the wind blew frostily from the north. It was almost an hour before the poor shivering wretches were allowed to replace their rifled garments on their limbs, now blue with cold. And when they did so, they found that all their money had been taken from them. A few Testaments which had been found on some of them were burned in a corner of the yard, and many were glad enough to warm their hands at the flame. Most of the chain consisted of thieves and murderers, and dire was the curse which these villains breathed against the Huguenot who had provoked the anger of the chief officer. He had taken a revenge judiciously contrived to wound a tender part. The sieur stood silent, and his eyes were lifted to a light that twinkled far away, midway between heaven and earth—he knew that his daughter was there, within a very few miles of him. It was the lights of St. Michel he gazed upon, but it was to no earthly potentate he bowed himself in submissive prayer that night.

The next morning they left their litter of straw at an early hour, *en route* for Dol; but of the convicts three were obliged to be deserted before they had marched three miles. The exposure of last night, added to their former sufferings and privations, had brought on congestion of the lungs; and, as the captain of the archers remarked when he ordered them to be set free, it was more humane to let the poor wretches die on the greensward in their own good time than to drag them moribund along the stony track. But the Sieur de Cornelli read in their mournful faces a reproach for having angrily addressed the officer, and he felt as if death would be a boon to him too.

They were on the confines of Brittany now, and the wild forest-land usurped the country on all sides. Herds of wild boar had left their recent tracks in the soft morass; the howling of wolves which had been their music through the night had ceased with the dawn, and a deathlike silence prevailed in the land through which the red-coated convicts were marching. The roads, too, were so villainous that it was no uncommon thing for the chain to be detained whilst one or more of its members floundered on the ground, and on such occasions the lash of one of the drivers was applied to help the fallen man quickly to his feet. By the *corvée*, or feudal rule, every tenant-farmer was obliged to send his labourers for so many days a year to assist in repairing the roads; but the king's necessities had already drafted the labourers into other fields, of sanguinary memories, and the farmers, having no men to work for them,

and heavier taxes to pay each year, had one by
one sunk into the slough of insolvency, sold
their chattels for an old song, and left the
untilled farms to the great game, the boars and
the wolves of Messieurs les Seigneurs.

The sight of such desolation and misery
recalled the Sieur de Cornelli from his own
private misfortunes; there was something in
the idea of his misfortunes being only part of
the general calamity which gave him spirit
to bear manfully up. In community of grief
there is a solace; one stricken heart gathers
strength from the sympathy of another, and
if there be possible no inter-communication of
expressed and conscious fellow-feeling, yet
some such spiritual relief is afforded by felt
sympathy with an absent friend as the soul
gathers from communion with the Eternal.
And the sieur had both the lesser and the
greater communion; for his heart had been
lifted up on the waves of suffering nearer
Heaven than it had ever been before, and the
sea of trouble becomes a pathway of holiness
when you find that Christ is walking beside
you on the waves.

There were, however, at every turn new
trials to surmount, new experiences of shame

and contumely to undergo. When they passed
through the little town of Dol, the inhabitants
came running out of their houses to look at the
convicts, and many of the women cursed the
Huguenots and spat in their faces, believing,
as they had been taught by their priests, that
these heretics worshipped the devil and prac-
tised all the deadly sins. But when they all
knelt down in the market-place and began to
sing one of their weird, pathetic hymns, those
who had gibed at them slank away, and two or
three young women offered them water to drink
and a crust of dry bread. It was the same thing
over again in every village where they stopped,
until they reached St. Malo, where the people
were used to the sight of the red coats, and
gave only a passing glance.

That night they were lodged in some stables,
for the galley *La Favorite* was not yet ready
for their reception. Before they went to sleep,
a novice of the Jesuit college came in to preach
to the convicts, taking as his text the words,
"Come unto Me, all ye who are weary and
heavy laden, and I will give you rest." The
substance of his discourse was that the Saviour,
in the words of this text, taught that one could
only come to Him by auricular confession. This

novice, both in coming in and going out of the
stables, made a great détour to avoid the
Huguenots, for he had been told that they were
all dangerous Huguenot ministers, and quite
capable of entrapping good Catholics. After
him came several Jesuit fathers to confess the
convicts, bringing with them the holy sacrament,
which they made them receive in a row, kneeling on their knees. The Huguenots sat
huddled up in a corner of the building, some
averting their eyes in horror, some quietly
engaged in silent prayer.

De Cornelli was watching the proceedings of
the Jesuits, and he remarked with surprise how,
after the priests had given them the Host, they
made them drink some wine out of a chalice.
So when all had retired for the night he made
bold to ask one of the convicts, a young man
who had been convicted of fighting a duel, if he
had received the communion in both kinds.

"Non, mon ami, non!" replied the youth,
"the wine in yon chalice was not consecrated;
it is only a precaution which the priests take
to make us swallow the Host. There is a
story which I have heard of a wicked galley-
slave who had made a compact with the devil,
that if he would release them all, he would

give him a consecrated wafer, which he therefore kept in his mouth for that purpose. The
galley-slave gave it to him, and on the journey
the whole chain was set at liberty by the Evil
One!"

There was a murmur of applause, which died
away in the clanking of chains as the unfortunate wretches turned over to seek sleep.

The next day they were distributed amongst
the several galleys which lay at anchor off the
town. The commander of *La Favorite* was a
short, stout man, with a red face fired by
alcohol; he growled at the idea of taking new
convicts, whom it was necessary to teach anew
by blows. The sieur was stripped to the waist,
and a chain was placed about his leg, by which
he was secured to his bench. As he was a tall
and powerful man, he was made strokesman and
placed in the first class.

There are six convicts to each oar, and the
strongest and most vigorous is made strokesman and has the hardest work. He is of the
first class, the next is second class, and so on
till the sixth class. The last has scarcely any
work, so the weakest and feeblest on the bench
is placed there. The galley-slave eats, drinks,
and sleeps on the same bench, and, in fact, he

may never be unchained for years. He is
stripped naked to the middle, and his hair is cut
short. A galley will hold from four hundred
to five hundred men, including fighting-men.
Under the commander is the *comite*, or mate,
who again has a *sous-comite*, or second mate,
under him. The under officer, charged with
guarding the galley-slaves, is styled the *argousin;* it is he who rivets the links which
attach the convicts to the benches. Besides
these, there are two or three muscular Turks,
whose duty it is to scourge the backs of those
whom the comite thinks worthy of punishment.
The comite himself eats and sleeps on a bench
of the galley, upon which a table, standing on
four little iron legs, is erected, and this table is
both long enough for him to take his meals at,
and also to spread his bed upon, being surrounded by a tent of coarse cotton cloth ; so
that the convicts of this bench are under the
table, which can easily be removed when they
want to row or perform any other manœuvre.
The six convicts of this bench form the
domestic establishment of the comite. Each
has his special employment in waiting upon
him, and when the comite takes his meals, all
the convicts of this bench, and of the benches

on each side, always stand up out of respect, with heads uncovered. It is the great ambition of all the convicts in the galley to be on the bench of the comite, and of the sous-comite, not only because they eat the remnants of their meals, but principally because they never get any stroke of the lash there while they are rowing; so these benches are called " reserved seats."

The sieur had not been long on board *La Favorite* when the chaplain came on board and began to inquire for him by name. This chaplain was a secular priest of St. Lazarus, an order founded by St. Vincent de Paul, and amongst whose many privileges and preroga- tives was that of nominating to the military, naval, and galley chaplaincies. He approached the bench on which De Cornelli was sitting, expressed his sorrow to see one so distin- guished in such a position, and pulling out of his pocket a letter, read an extract which com- mended the Sieur de Cornelli to Father Garcin's care and attention.

"You will readily conjecture," he added, "that it is le Père Beretti who has written this letter; and I therefore begin by ordering the argousin to take off that heavy fetter and remove you to the bench of the comite."

Accordingly this was done, and the sieur expressed his thanks to the chaplain.   But when
he was conversing with the father, a movement
of the crew made him turn towards the other
side of the galley, where the sous-comite was
busy strapping to the bench, with his face down-
wards, a grey-haired convict who neither spoke
nor made any resistance.   A strong-built Turk
was standing by with a thick rope, and at a
given signal he began to belabour the bare
back of the wretched galley-slave, and whenever the Turk struck feebly, the sous-comite
freshened him up with a smart blow of his whip.

"What is that for?" said the sieur to Father
Garcin.

"Oh! it is only an old offender getting a
salad of strokes for blaspheming against the
Catholic religion—he richly deserves fifty, but
he is to have only twenty.   You will see the
barber-surgeon come and rub his back with
strong vinegar and salt soon."

"What barbarity!" murmured De Cornelli.

"Point du tout! you do not know the art,
monsieur.   This after-process is of a beneficial
character, namely, to prevent gangrene from
coming on.   The back of that miserable old
man would else fail to regain its sensibility."

The sieur turned away with horror from the mass of bleeding, lacerated flesh.

"Who may that old man be in whom you take so kindly an interest?" he asked ironically.

The priest replied, "Only a pasteur from Normandy—La Rose, they name him."

"La Rose!" shouted the sieur, almost fiercely.

"Pourquoi non!" replied Father Garcin, taking a pinch of snuff daintily between his finger and thumb.

De Cornelli stood up on his bench to examine the face of the pasteur, who was about to undergo the salt and vinegar. Then, when he was convinced that it was his old friend of Coutances, he cried out—

"There has been some mistake in punishing that old man. Send Monsieur de Maulevrier to me; I must speak to the captain immediately!"

The comite turned fiercely on the sieur.

"Dog of a Huguenot, hold your tongue! Remember you are now a slave—*my* slave; and I will cut your skin to ribands if you dare to make a hubbub about this paltry flogging."

The Captain De Maulevrier hearing the altercation, and seeing de Cornelli standing in a threatening attitude, came running down the *coursier*, a gangway which passes down the middle of the galley from one end to the other, and is about four feet broad.

"Ventrebleu! eh! par la mort! get down, sirrah! What! are you going to head a rebellion in my galley? Holà! Send the Turk hither!" And the executioner crossed over to the sieur's side of the galley, holding in his hand the blood-stained rope with which he had flogged the pasteur.

"Now, sirrah," shouted the choleric captain, "what is the cause of this disorder?"

"The Chevalier de Maulevrier does me wrong in accusing me of a wish to resist his authority," answered the sieur; "God knows it were useless, even if it were my intention! But, seeing an old friend unjustly flogged, I could not but lift my voice; for the king, I am sure, deems the punishment of the galleys enough, without needless and cruel floggings."

"Haughty language this, for a slave! How know you the bastinado was not deserved?"

"By my knowledge of yon old man's character. I will answer for his innocence by my life; question those who sit near him, and see what they say of his conduct."

The captain could not meet the straight-
forward, unflinching glance of the sieur; he
turned on his heel, muttering an oath. "Who
accuses the old man?" sharply he asked the
comite. The latter pointed to a convict who
was lying on his bench, rolled up in his cloak,
and apparently asleep. At a signal from the
captain the Turk hit him smartly on the head
with the end of his rope, and to the great
surprise of De Cornelli, when the man turned
round and showed his face, it was no other than
that of Brother Francis, the Benedictine.

The red, ferret eyes glittered angrily, and the
pock-marked cheeks grew hot as the captain
proceeded to question him. He had heard the
pasteur revile the Blessed Virgin and mock at
the mass, he said; but the convicts on either
side denied his statement, and there were some
who were not Huguenots who testified in the
old man's favour.

"Now which am I to believe?" said the
captain, with an oath.

"By your permission," said De Cornelli, "I
can tell you something about yon Benedictine
which may help to decide you." And he narrated
the part which Brother Francis had taken in
persecuting his Catholic wife.

"Strap him down to his bench," cried the captain, as soon as he had heard the story; "strap him down and get out a new rope. Why, the rascal only came on board yesterday, pleading that he had vowed to do a week's penance as a galley-slave, and would I be so kind as to give him a seat! Oui, oui, mon ami, I will give you such a seat as will find you in penance for a year to come! Oh! you need not whimper like a cursed puppy; give him twenty-five for his false accusations, and twenty-five with the compliments of Monseigneur le Sieur de Cornelli."

Father Garcin tapped the lid of his snuff-box. "C'est assez drole-çà."

But De Cornelli said—"Stay one moment, Monsieur le Capitaine. I do not wish to plead for any remission of punishment for the offence of lying against my poor friend there—a few strokes may do the monk some real good, and awaken his conscience—but I do want you to pardon him the remaining twenty-five; for I assure him that, though he has robbed me of all that I held dearest, I do not bear him malice, believing that he acted in ignorance, obeying the laws of a false *esprit de corps*."

The captain stood a moment astonished; at last he yelled out—

" Do you hear, monk ? he bears you no
malice ! He ought to be ashamed of himself !
If you had killed my wife and child, I would
have pursued you with malice to the grave, le
maudit ! Holà, Monsieur le Comite ! withhold
the latter twenty-five lashes from the seigneur,
but let him have instead fifty additional strokes
in the name of Justice."

There was a murmur of applause as the captain's sentence was given out. But the seventy-
five blows were not given without the Turk's
needing a salad of strokes, as the chaplain
termed it, to encourage him to greater vigour ;
and not all the salt and vinegar that was applied
could at once restore feeling to the lacerated
back of the unhappy monk.

And so passed the sieur's first day in his
Majesty's galley. In less than a week he had so
won the good opinion of the captain that he
was promoted to the post of secretary, and from
the bench under the table of the comite was
transferred to the captain's cabin, where he en-
joyed tolerable tranquillity, when that gentleman
was not drunk.

CHAPTER XI.

IN a low-roofed chamber of the abbey of Mont
St. Michel, Father Beretti was sitting by the
bedside of Du Hamel, who lay with his head in
bandages, looking very pale and miserable.
The dark, handsome face of the Jesuit was
slightly turned away from the wounded boy,
his black, searching eyes were fixed upon the
blank wall beyond, and as the confession poured
forth in faltering words, the confessor seemed
only half conscious of their meaning; the other
half of his attention was arrested by an inner
stream of thoughts suggested by Du Hamel's
narration. But when the latter ceased speaking, Father Beretti gently pressed the hand
which lay in his, and murmured a few words of
consolation, with one of his bewitching smiles,
which the ladies of St. Germains had found so
irresistible. Then he shook up the pillow and

smoothed the bed-clothes as tenderly as any
woman could have done it, and whispered, before
he left the chamber—

"Adieu, mon fils! I will ask the ladies to
visit you;" but when the lieutenant made a
little grimace, added, "A good heart! Mademoiselle De Cornelli shall come alone, and you
shall confide your trouble to her. Who knows
but what she may explain away the circumstances which wound your heart? Adieu,
adieu!"

The Jesuit passed through the salle des
chevaliers, then, turning to the left, he traversed
the refectory of the monks, and so into the
" crypte des gros piliers," which support the
entire weight of the church above. There he
knelt for a few minutes before a statue of the
black Madonna, absorbed in silent prayer. He
did not notice a friar who stood patiently behind
him with a packet of letters in his hand, waiting
until his orison was finished.

" The messenger from Pontorson has returned
with letters from the king's posts," said the friar,
humbly bowing as he tendered the papers.

" Bene est; tu, frater, velim abeas."

The friar bowed again and retired.

Beretti passed on until he came to the

Chapel St. Etienne, and, descending one of
the numerous rock staircases, found his way to
his own private apartment, lit by a narrow
aperture cut out of the rock. Here he lighted
his lamp and sat down to examine the papers
which had just arrived from Pontorson. They
were not all for him, since it seemed he had
given orders that all letters for Marie and
Ethel should be brought to him first.

"À Monsieur Dubourg," he read aloud,
holding up to the light a sealed letter; "le
pauvre vieux! he has been so long in the iron
cage that letters have no charm for him." Then,
breaking the seal and reading, "Five thousand
livres—his absolute use. Mon Dieu! were he
set free to-morrow he could not enjoy a sou
of it!"

Another letter was next taken up. "Ah,
enfin! the sieur writes from St. Malo. Mais,
comment! the Benedictine discovered in the
same galley, gives false evidence against the
pasteur, receives the bastinado! Ah, l'infâme!
then he has received his merits! Pray God
I may never pollute His holy cause by descending to base and immoral measures. Poor
brother! thou wert a fine, earnest boy-student,
and now what hast thou become?—a murderer,

a liar, a diabolus ! ' Un petit mal pour un grand
bien,' that used to be thy doctrine, and ' Dieu
se sert de tous les moyens.' Ah, mon Dieu !
what dirty deeds are done in Thy name ! And
yet I know not if some of our casuists do not
tend in that way ; we are over-impatient, and
cannot wait for the ways of Providence, but
must needs be hurrying on by our own muddy
bye-paths. Mais à propos ! am I right in detain-
ing this letter from mademoiselle ? My superior
bids me keep her in ignorance of her father's
place of detention, and obedience is my first
law ; if I show her this letter she will learn
all. They seem to fear an attempt at rescue in
thus keeping him in secret, n'est-ce-pas ? or
perhaps the authorities wish to avoid any repeated petitions for his .release, mine having
signally failed ? Ah, there comes in the cursed
love of lands. That Maintenon !—hypocritical
harlot that hast turned against thy own religion
for an ecclesiastical sanction to thy concubin-
age !—it is thy greed and thy brother's that
keeps the fetters of the sieur fast riveted ! But
I must set my new plot a-working. Ha, ha !
it will go ill with me if I do not shake the
false image from Marie's shrine with this boy's
jealous tale."

So, chuckling to himself, Father Beretti went to the lady-superior who had succeeded the Abbess of Fontevraud, and asked her to persuade Marie to go with one of the sisters to visit the wounded officer.

Marie and Ethel were now very dull. The abbey had grown *triste* since the Abbé Huet and Sister Gabrielle had gone, and Du Hamel no longer afforded them cause for merriment; and Marie had had no letter from her father for a long time, and no news of Henri and Philippe, and the Comte de Pontorson was continually riding over to bore her with his vinous courtesies. Accordingly, when the lady-superior suggested a visit to Du Hamel under her guidance, she caught at it as a relief from a long monotony.

Ethel was away, visiting some sick poor with two of the sisters amongst the cabins that stood behind the tamarisks on the shore, and Marie had grown pensive over the " Fleurs des Saints," and was wishing herself espoused to the religious life, when the little plain-faced nun came in and dispelled her sick dreams with matter-of-fact inquiries.

Why was mademoiselle alone ? Had she received the white wool for her knitting ?

When would Mademoiselle l'Anglaise return ?
Such and similar questions, put in a sharp,
impatient tone of voice, quickly recalled her to
the world of petty annoyances, and reminded
her that the *religieuse*, when she shut the door
of her convent, no more shut out her earth-born
frailties than she did her shadow.

The lieutenant's pale face was suffused with
a boyish blush when the rustle of dresses and
the sight of Marie's piquante figure made him
half expect the appearance of Ethel ; for since
his duel he had brooded over the events of that
night with the warm imagination of a lover,
and the causes which he had for jealousy only
fanned the flames which were consuming him.
And yet he dare not meet her face, lest she
should dash the glimmer of hope which still
danced like an *ignis fatuus* before him, by
declaring that she loved not him, but another.

The nun did not long remain by his bedside,
but, leaving the door ajar, set herself in the
next room and plied her long needles with
noisy rapidity. Marie took the chair which
had lately been occupied by Beretti, and began
to read aloud. Either the plaintive tenderness
of her voice, or the pathos of the story she was
reading, or the weak health of Du Hamel, or

perhaps all three combined, started the tears
from his eyes, and Marie, glancing up from her
book, saw them rolling down his cheeks.

"Do I weary you, monsieur?" she cried,
letting the volume fall upon her lap.

"Oh, non, madame! but your way of reading
made me remember my sorrow."

Marie started. Sorrow! could she not pour
balm into the wounds of this poor boy? He
seemed to wish for some one in whom to confide his troubles, so Marie leaned over him and
said—"If you wish to tell me your grief, I will
share it with you, mon frère." And as she
spoke, she felt instinctively that it was about
Ethel he would talk.

He gazed upon her timidly, trying to read
in her face the signs of sympathy, before he
ventured to open his lips on a matter so sacred
to him.

"You will think me foolish, I know," he
began, "but I cannot help loving the English
lady, in spite of all her efforts to shake me off.
Vous voyez, mademoiselle, there is not a trooper
in our regiment can ride with greater ease
than she; and with a pistol she can cleave a
nail's head at twenty paces. I have seen her
do it! Then that beautiful long fair hair!

Oh! that by itself is enough to turn a soldier's head, especially when, as I have seen it do, it escapes from its chains and flows rippling down her shoulders. Ah, mademoiselle! your brown, wavy hair is pretty, but hers is the hair of a goddess!"

Marie began to think that the conversation was scarcely edifying, and the more because Du Hamel had only just come away from death's door, at which he had been knocking feverishly for seven days. Decidedly it needed a religious turn; so she gave it one.

"Has not the father confessor just been to see you? Surely you did not talk to him in so light a strain, and if I am to do you any good service, it must be by directing your thoughts to higher things."

"Oh, please not to attempt it! My head is too painful for 'higher things,'" answered the alarmed officer, in a piteous tone of entreaty.

"Fi donc, monsieur! if your head is light, I am wasting my time. Let me, however, give you some good advice: when a woman says she is averse to you, slight her, neglect her, make as though you cared not a brass nail whether she loved you or no! You are too hot after Mistress Ethel. Pardieu! use my prescription, and I will not guarantee the quality of her ice-cold courtesy for longer than the waning of a moon!"

"Nay! I know she loves me not; my faith has been rudely broken."

"Because, mon frère, you have trusted in yourself. You have not asked a blessing on your endeavours; and for you the rustle of no angel wing makes the soul quiver at the presence of the Spirit of God."

"Oh, parfaitement, madame! I have prayed, vowed, and done grievous penance to catch her smiles; but I lost all heart when I found she loved another."

"Loved another!" ejaculated Marie.

"It is too certain! I saw him kiss her hand the other night."

"Who? when? what can you mean?" cried Marie, in a sudden impatience; and the arching eyebrows seemed to close together and ask counsel of one another, making a pretty, piteous corrugation on the delicate surface of her brow. "Dites moi, monsieur, whom did you see?"

"It was the night you found me out beyond the walls. I had noticed la belle Anglaise pass down the street with Lisette, closely hooded and masked; I followed in a blind fit of jealousy, for I suspected how it was. They entered the hostel in the Cour du Lion, and I wrapped myself up in my cloak and waited under the archway. Shortly a light shot across the road; I knew that the door was opening, and hurried past to catch a glimpse of the person whom she had gone to visit, without myself attracting attention.

" And you saw ? "

" I saw a young man, well-made, with dark hair and eyes, and a dimple in his cursed smiling cheeks; he was just stooping to kiss her hand, and——"

" And she, monsieur ? "

" Ah, mon Dieu! she shot a glance of affection from her false, blue eyes, and said, in a tender, melancholy tone, 'Soyez heureux—the next time we meet under happier auspices;' and he bowed and came away. And then, you know, I dogged his steps till he reached the rocks under St. Aubert's Well, where I challenged him to fight, for I saw he carried a sword. And indeed, methought once he was the English sailor who stole away from us some weeks ago; but, le maudit! he fenced like no Englishman, or I should have pricked him under the fifth rib, instead of getting this ugly slash on the

head, with his polite, 'Vous voilà, monsieur, et
bon soir!' which I heard ere my consciousness
left me."

"Mais, monsieur," said Marie, struggling
against an uncomfortable feeling, a sort of a
suspicion which Du Hamel's words had evoked
in her, "does not thy jealousy twist words and
deeds to its own yellow interpretation?—thou
knowest that a man may kiss a lady's hand in
courtesy."

"So I would have persuaded myself, but
Lisette, whom I sent for to question on what
passed within, hath told me that which put an
end to all doubt; but the closeness of this
chamber affects thee somewhat, I fear."

Marie tried to reply "No," but her tongue
failed her, and a sudden spasm made her place
her hand to her heart; she turned deadly pale.
Du Hamel now raised his voice, and the nun
came running in just in time to support Marie
out of the chamber. And this is what came of
Marie's first attempt to play the sister and pour
in precious balm.

She left the room with a thousand wild
emotions stirring the heart which had been
espoused, in intent and purpose, to conventual
tranquillity. At a less startling crisis of her

spiritual life she would have just glided like a ghost into the silent church, and knelt before the presence of St. Michel and beneath the motionless banners that hung as votive offerings from the walls; but now she seized her hood and sallied out alone into the street, scarce knowing whom or what she was seeking. Three sisters carrying baskets of broken victuals met her half way down the road, and accosted her; but she hardly noticed them as she hurried by with parted lips and a blanched cheek. One of these followed her, as it was an unheard-of thing for her to go forth alone.

"Pardon me," she said, touching her on the arm; "can I help you in your quest, for you seem hurried."

"Merci," whispered Marie, "I go alone; I seek speech with Lisette."

The sister, however, followed her, for unknown to Marie an order had been given that she was never to be suffered to go from the convent unattended. As they passed through the Cour du Lion, as the narrow space was called between the outer and second gate, Marie asked a girl who was sitting astride of the Michelette, one of the cannon which had been taken from the English in 1427, whether Lisette

were at home, and receiving a shake of the head
for a reply—for the girl's mouth was too dis-
tended by a crust of bread for utterance—she
hurried on through the Bavolle, or *porte de
ville*, through which she could see a group of
women clustered on the sands.

The women of St. Michel were in the habit
of going out *en masse* upon an excursion in
quest of shell-fish, crabs, mollusks, and what else
they could extract from the grip of the grey
desert. They were provided with long poles, in
case any of their number should be unlucky
enough to fall into the quicksands, when a line
was formed by the rest joining hands, and the
poles were laid on the surface on the sand. To-
day they had just returned from such an ex-
pedition, and were busy turning out the spoil of
the morning from their sacks upon the flat rocks
which lay without the wall, whilst two or three
fishermen, husbands or fathers, stood admiring,
with hands thrust deep in their pockets and the
tassels of their red caps hanging jauntily over
one shoulder.

Marie ran her eye swiftly over the group, in
the hope of catching sight of Lisette. An in-
congruous crowd they looked, as they jabbered
and gesticulated with a fierceness which seemed

quite uncalled-for, around the little heaps of shell-fish which were to supply the town with its daily relish. All wore their dresses looped up above the knee ; some wore their husbands' thick coats over their dresses, some wore tarpaulin hats, and some a red kerchief tied under the chin. But what looked most grotesque was the strange assemblage of naked legs and feet which presented itself then, as now, to the beholder. Legs in which there was unity as well as variety—unity of colour, for they were all tingling red from toe to thigh with the salt water ; variety of size and form, for there were the shrunk spindle-shanks of the grey-haired *grandmère*, the swollen calves of the buxom matron, and the graceful, rounded limbs of the girl, in close contraposition ; and such an assortment of toes as is only vouchsafed in modern days to the professional corn-cutter—toes curling upwards with unexpected levity, toes coiling over their fellows, as though they were privileged to take a familiarity with their next-door neighbours, toes writhing in pitiful contortions, toes short and toes long, all trampling the grey sand in the rosy livery which they had caught from a long immersion in the salt creeks ; and lastly, the straight, finger-like toes of the little girls whose pretty feet had never been caged in wooden *sabots*. But amongst all these pink legs and multiform feet none bore the buoyant figure of the black-eyed, olive-skinned Lisette. But to Marie's inquiry, "Où donc est Lisette?" a laughing-eyed maiden pointed to a piece of fallen rock, and behind this Marie found the girl she sought standing beside Gustave, who was sorting her spoil for her, and putting the edible shells into an earthenware jar.

Lisette was standing with one arm akimbo and her head slightly inclined on the same side, observing the mollusks with the air of a connoisseur. The heel of her right foot was resting on the instep of the left, and as she stood poised in this natural attitude she was a study that Phidias would have envied. For the girl, with pardonable vanity, seldom cramped her feet with the cruel *sabots*, and her firm, rounded limbs preserved their pale olive tint through the delicate pink engendered by the cold.

The presence of Gustave was embarrassing in the extreme. Marie stood before them with a troubled air of bewilderment, and could find nothing to say to explain her hurried approach. But the honest-hearted giant divined her un-spoken wishes, and, telling Lisette he would be

back shortly, made as though he had gone to
fetch another pail for the fish. The sister who
had followed Marie was conversing with the
fish-wives at a distance, still keeping her eye on
the demoiselle, and so Marie and Lisette were
alone.

"Gustave is very foolish, to be sure, to run
away just now ; and all because he is afraid of
you, mademoiselle," said Lisette, pouting.

"He afraid of poor me ! I am not so fine a
lady of quality."

"Non, malheureusement, non ! we heard it
to-day, mademoiselle, and I am very sorry
indeed for you, and so are we all."

"Heard what, Lisette ? I do not understand,"
said Marie, starting.

"Ah ! they say bad news flies in the air,
while good news paces afoot ! It was monsieur
là-bas, the grand forester of Monsieur le Comte,
who told us."

"Told you what ? I have heard no news,
good or bad. What said he ? "

"Mon Dieu ! non ? est-il possible ? I would
not have spoken of it had I thought that
mademoiselle did not know it. Est-il possible ? Voyez vous, mademoiselle, monsieur the
forester began to tease me about my eyes,

forsooth, and I needs must ask him in return
whether he thought himself as true a lover as
his master. 'God save the mark!' quoth he;
'my master's love has been blown out.' 'How
so?' quoth I. 'Have you not heard,' saith he,
'that all the estates of the De Cornelli have
been declared forfeit, and that a grand courtier
has bought them up cheap?' 'And what of
that, monsieur?' said I, in my simplicity. 'Why,
you little fool,' said the grand forester, 'Monsieur le Comte de Pontorson is not the man to
marry a girl without a dowry; he wants money
too sorely for that.' 'Whew!' said I, 'is that
it?—then I fear mademoiselle will die a maid,
after all.'"

Marie smiled haughtily at the girl, who had
retailed the foregoing conversation with a certain
spice of malice. Her pride was touched by the
half-sneering way in which Lisette had spoken,
though, as she knew, it sprang from the extreme childishness of her mind, and was beneath
her notice. But the moment she knew that
the advantages of wealth and social position
had been taken from her, all the ancestral pride
of race welled up in her bosom, lent colour to
her cheek, fire to her eye, and tipped her tongue
with aristocratic scorn.

"Pardon, madame," said Lisette, apologetically, when she observed the effect of her words, "I did not mean to offend."

"Oh! it is nothing to speak of. As for my wealth, I shall not miss it, for I intend to enter a nunnery. As for Monsieur le Comte, I shall be only too glad to be free from his importunity."

"Vraiment! and he a Chevalier of the Order, too! Hé bien! we cannot all be saints and martyrs, that is one comfort. Then there is Mademoiselle l'Anglaise; she cannot become a sister too, for she is a heretic, they say. Ah! I should not wonder if she were to marry the lieutenant of marines."

Marie shivered; this was cutting her to the marrow. She asked, with a sickness of heart which argued ill for her conventual peace of mind—

"What idle talk is this, Lisette? What lieutenant meanest thou?"

Lisette, a little nettled by her tone, replied consequentially—

"Mademoiselle thinks Lisette knows nothing; she is a poor peasant girl, and, *sans doute*, has no eyes beyond her fish-basket. But I can tell you that when I was at the abbey school

Monsieur le Curé praised my curiosity—'thirst for knowledge,' he called it ; and, indeed, I do manage to see what my neighbours are doing as well as most girls of my standing."

" Oh ! I do not doubt it. Have with you there, for as sly a cat as ever watched a mouse ! But what, my good Lisette, have you seen, now ? " The brunette took Marie's words as complimentary, and replied confidentially—

" Why, he who comes under cover of night to see mademoiselle—the lieutenant of marines, whom I have known ever so long up yonder at Avranches. He is in love with the Anglaise, as all the world may see."

Marie began to breathe more freely ; if she had nothing but Henri's visits to go by, the story was soon explained. Lisette continued—

" I watched them the other night. In the first place, when I returned from the abbey and said that you, mademoiselle, would not come, but that Mademoiselle Ethel was with me, he seemed much moved. I was obliged to repeat it to him twice, and tell him your exact words."

Marie smiled. The interpretation ran fair so far.

" Et puis, they sat by the fire and talked, while I peeled apples and listened. I can't remember all they said, but he kept looking up in her face admiringly, as I thought. And the wind had blown the roses into her cheeks; I don't wonder at him for it. Then she said something low, and finished off with 'monsieur,' very distantly courteous, to which he replied that she must not address him now as 'monsieur,' but as 'Henri.'"

"Nay, good Lisette, 'tis a good story! But what said she to that?"

"Oh! she smiled and toyed with her gold chain, and at last, when he pleaded with her, whispered that perhaps she would call him 'Henri' some day. And so they parted, he kissing her hand at the door; and coming back to the fire, he sighed so fiercely I thought I must have laughed outright."

"And how looked they, Lisette?—as lovers are wont to do?"

"Oui, oui, certainement! I am sorry for Monsieur du Hamel yonder, because he is frantic for Mademoiselle l'Anglaise; all the men love her, she rides so well. I would, mademoiselle, some gallant might please you!"

Marie, driven by the yellow-faced fiend Jealousy to drink of the waters of scandal, felt that she had degraded herself in Lisette's eyes and before the bar of her own conscience. The random talk of the thoughtless girl had hit home and driven the barb of suspicion deeper into her heart. As she turned away, in the very gall of bitterness, she reflected that to offer to Christ a heart which had been spurned by a man was an insult, a sacrilege. For the moment, the night of despair, a sense of utter loneliness, settled upon her. All love seemed to have been cruelly taken from her. Father, mother, brother, torn away, and their memories clouded by their sufferings ; friendship had proved false, love had changed to hate and jealousy ; and, to crown all, the feeling that there were spirits above to whom she could unbosom her sorrows, and in whom she could find peace and comfort, had been made impossible to her. She could not tell you why, but her heart had grown suddenly cold and unheavenly. She saw no Virgin Mother sitting beside the gracious Son. There was a veil drawn over the eye of faith. She felt she had done wrong, though where the sin commenced, and how to analyze it, she knew not. Heaven and earth were alike unjust. If she had prayed, her petitions would have curdled into reproaches ere they reached the throne of God.

As she drew near the gate of the town,
Ethel was just returning with two of the nuns
from visiting some sick folk on the shore. Ethel
had quickened her pace when she saw Marie
pause as if waiting her approach, but to her surprise noticed that her friend turned away from
her and hurried home. It was the first step in
the withdrawal of sympathy. Marie was far
too proud ever to allude to what Lisette had
told her, much less to nurse any spiteful feeling
against Ethel ; but she could not help despising
her in her heart for doing a mean thing in winning Henri's affections, and she could not help
showing a certain coldness of manner towards
her, which had been quite foreign to her nature
hitherto.

Ethel would sometimes lie awake and wonder
what had come over her friend ; but she finally
put it down to Marie's religious views and ever
increasing austerity of worship. And though
she deeply pitied the poor motherless girl, who
would kneel for hours in the church and come
away sadder and paler than ever, yet, somehow,
she never ventured to intrude 'her robuster
thoughts into the sickly atmosphere of Marie's
religious life. They differed so widely on such
points that no sympathy seemed possible.

And so the winter months wore on, and the spring returned and visited the Abbé Huet's flowers, and yet no letter came from the sieur, nor from Henri, nor from Philippe; at least not to Marie, for le Père Beretti, after reading them, had locked them up "ad majorem Deo gloriam."

And so Marie thought her father had been taken to Paris, and thence to the southern shore, to Marseilles, or one other of the ports where the king's galleys lay; and when sometimes she watched the boats from St. Malo rowing across the smooth bay, she would think to herself—"Ah me! my poor father is prisoned in such a galley as that!" How she would have started could one have whispered to her, "Yes, maiden; yonder goes the galley in which thy father slaves!" But happily, perhaps, for her, she knew not.

Father Beretti was week by week fashioning her to the new life of meditation and self-surrender, and the need of some object on whom to lavish her love made Marie yield to the fascinating address of the handsome Jesuit. She shared her heart henceforth equally between an ideal Christ and an idealized confessor. Woman must have some idol, something not abstract, not pure spirit, to found her heart upon. And Marie built up her faith on the best man she knew, the tenderest next to her own father, the most unselfish, the most spiritual, le Père Beretti. And he—the petted confessor of the Jesuit Church in the Rue St. Antoine; he, who had shown himself proof against all merely human feelings, and had volunteered to serve in the provinces—could not help his heart throbbing with more than spiritual joy, as he whispered to himself—

" I shall make a saint of that girl. Deo gloriam ! "

But the end was not yet.

CHAPTER XII.

THE unfortunate Du Hamel remained long confined to his couch, for sorrow and despondency
are not good bed-fellows to sickness; and
though Marie would sometimes come and read
to him, attended by one of the sisters, he never
once asked to see Ethel, nor did he and Marie
recur to the painful theme which was rendering
them both unhappy. Before he was strong
enough to walk about the abbey, his uncle, a
man celebrated for his learning and of considerable means, removed him to his own home.
He would have gone away without saying
good-bye to Ethel; but she was standing in
the *salle des gardes* as he passed, and, indeed,
pushed her way through the crowd of soldiers
and servants to press his hand. The men who
bore his litter stood still, and Ethel, breaking

through her natural shyness, stammered out,
with a deep blush that crept from her forehead
far down her neck beyond the ken of propriety—

"Bon voyage! may you return stronger—
and more full of life and hope—adieu!" And
with these words ringing in his ears, the lieutenant was borne between the two rows of
dragoons who lined the gateway to honour his
departure.

Ethel shot an angry glance of indignant
pride at the women, who were whispering some
audible comment on her changing colour, and
soon forgot, or seemed to forget, in the active
life she led amongst the fishermen and peasantry on the coast, all memory of her dis-
appointed lover.

And Marie grew more meditative, and her
complexion grew more delicate, and her cheeks,
like pearls, seemed to grow more tenderly
beautiful the more they were seen, and her long
dark eye-lashes were now not seldom sweeping
them with beads of sorrow.

"Elle est pieuse!" the nuns would say, as
she knelt in an ecstacy of devotion before the
high altar.

"Elle y arrivera!" murmured the Jesuit,

with folded arms, as he stood in the shadow of an archangel.

But Ethel sighed over the loss of a friend, and distrusting in her heart the fervour of this exaggerated passion of the soul, would some- times lead the conversation to Marie's mother and her active life of beneficence, and try to awake by this silent contrast the conscience of the melancholy-minded girl. But for the present Beretti was too strong; he had made up his mind that Marie was to be a " virgo Deo consecrata," as he phrased it, since the Comte de Pontorson's salvation could no longer be bought by the sacrifice of Mademoiselle de Cornelli.

And the summer of 1686 visited Mont St. Michel, bringing with it the usual crowds of holiday-seekers and pilgrims, and more crutches were suspended before the little black Virgin in the crypt, and more wives hastened home to hope for the crown of maternity. And one evening there was quite a house-full of people assembled in the little hostel in the Cour du Lion, where Monsieur le Curé sat sipping a cup of hypocras, and Lisette's eyes were sparkling with delight at the presents spread before her. And the notary-public from Pontorson put on his spectacles and witnessed the signatures of

Gustave and Lisette, and at midnight the wedded pair went with their friends to attend a midnight mass in the old church on the slope of the mount, and early next morning, before the newly wedded were up, a cake soaked in wine was carried to them by their most familiar friends, which they had to eat with such shame-faced solemnity as they could muster for the occasion. And after all this, Gustave and Lisette were regarded by the Montois as man and wife, and continued to live in the old hostel, and to do the duties of mine host, Lisette's father, who was too rheumatic to do anything but tell his beads.

And then the abbey relapsed into its usual routine. Ethel, however, found some interest, if not amusement, in the spiritual advances of the fathers who from time to time came to the abbey *en retraite;* for, as they succeeded one another at short intervals, there were few who did not think it incumbent on them to break a theologic lance with the golden-haired heretic. And as they were all men of sober years and generally of silver-haired discretion, Ethel did not mind when the discussion on points of doctrine branched off, as it often would, into good-natured quips or interesting peeps into the

personal experiences of these tonsured worthies,
many of whom were men of some learning, and
were glad enough to unbend their brows in the
artless society of the merry " belle Anglaise."
Sometimes, too, they would take rod and line
and wander beside the Coesnon, Ethel and one
of the sisters being of the party, while Gustave
pointed out the deep corners and favourite
haunts of the fish, and was ready to land in his
net any obstreperous trout that refused to leave
its native element.

And so September came again, and Beretti
was recalled to Paris, much to his personal
disgust ; for, really, the problem which he had
set himself to solve in analyzing and promoting
the development of Marie's spiritual life had
become so ingrossing, that to be called away
just when his care and surveillance were beginning to receive their reward was almost pro-
voking, even to a Jesuit. However, it is more
than probable that his superior knew as much,
if not more, about the spiritual problem which
he had set himself to develop, and determined,
however ruthlessly, to transport the young
enthusiast into a more busy life, a more bracing
atmosphere.

Scarcely had the inmates of the abbey had

time to recover from their regret at his departure, when the arrival of the Abbé Huet, and shortly after of Mère Gabrielle de Rochechouart, Abbess of Fontevraud, restored all to good humour and mirth. The little abbé rallied Marie on her pale cheeks and pensive mood, insisted upon her accompanying the others in their walks, told her so many anecdotes that the smiles came hovering about her lips, like young doves that have flown from their cage and, returning to it, half fear to enter. And so the wild sea-winds blustering about the face of this would-be nun, and the incisive common-sense utterances of this scholar among bishops, sent a cloud of strange distempered fancies from the poor girl's head, and braced her anew to meet the buffets and the shocks of time.

There was one subject upon which the good abbé was unable to throw any light, when Marie advised with him—he could not tell her where her father was detained; and though he addressed the chaplain of the abbey, and the governor of the fortress, and the curé of the parish, and the four or five aged sisters who resided in the conventual buildings, on the point in question, not one of them had ever been

able to extract from Père Beretti the name of
the port or galley in which the sieur was living.

They were sitting one afternoon in the
private apartment of "Sister Gabrielle," as she
chose to be named at Mont St. Michel; Marie
was reading aloud, seated on the floor by the
window, and Ethel and Sister Gabrielle were
working at some warm clothing for the poor,
when the abbé rushed into the room, his
spectacles in his hand, and his hair flying in
disorder.

"Pardon!" he gasped out; "I have seen
Mademoiselle Marie, attired like a peasant-girl,
walking in suspicious company near the gates."

"Pray calm yourself, monseigneur," replied
the lady abbess, in a tone half-soothing, half-
expostulating; "and trust your senses. Voilà
Mademoiselle Marie!"

The poor abbé, seeing the lady in question
quietly seated on the floor, was fairly embarrassed; he stood open-mouthed for some
seconds.

"I could swear I saw her five minutes ago
in the large bonnet and blue blouse of a
peasant; an apothecary, judging by his long
robe and square cap, accompanied her. Oh!
I could not mistake that face; the tint of the

flesh would have betrayed you, daughter, any-
where."

"Monseigneur must have the gift of second-
sight," said Sister Gabrielle, smiling at Ethel.
"Allons donc, mon ami, sit down and make
yourself some of your favourite Chinese
beverage, for you seem excited."

The abbé sat down, and as Ethel prepared
his tea, kept muttering to himself, "Second
sight, second sight—et pourquoi non?" and
presently, when the black wine of the east had
allayed his fever, he discoursed learnedly on
second sight and prophecy. "Who knows,
Mademoiselle Ethel, if after all Providence
may not have designed me to enter the lists
against your heretical prophet, Jurieu, and con-
found with a clearer prevision his commentaries
on the Apocalypse!"

"But," said Ethel, laughing, "you have begun
by making an egregious blunder, for Marie
was here all the time. I have heard 'that pro-
phecies shall fail,' and now I have a living
instance of the decadence thereof."

Huet sniffed angrily in the air, and answered
pettishly—

"I deny your minor. I deny the logical
inference that because mademoiselle was here,

therefore I was mistaken. I saw what will take place hereafter ! "

" Est-il possible ? " exclaimed Marie, opening her eyes wide with wonder.

"*Sans doute !* " cried Huet, gathering confidence from the girl's alarm ; " *sans doute !* The thing is borne in upon me with a strange, mysterious power. Such gifts are vouchsafed to men of—of—excuse me, daughters, if I seem to be egotistical—of unusual parts and subtle intelligence. It was only two years ago that a French nobleman, sitting on the stage of one of your English theatres, as the custom is, cried out with horror, as the Duke of Monmouth entered the pit, ' Voilà monsieur, comme il entre sans tête ! ' Twelve months after that the executioner was hacking at his neck ! Mon Dieu ! there is that in the mind of man which passeth man's philosophy to fathom."

" A strange story ! " said Sister Gabrielle. " Really, to be in your society, monseigneur, after coming from our hum-drum life at Fontevraud is very refreshing, and, in good sooth, almost too exhilarating for the tranquil nerves of a nun."

" Ah, daughter ! in that sweet retirement of yours you have not forgotten the graceful

flattery which so became the lips of Mademoiselle de Mortemar. I bethink me of what
our old friend Rochefoucald has said so finely,
'On croit quelquefois haïr la flatterie, mais on
ne hait que la maniere de flatter!' By the way,
I heard a good story about one of our famous
abbés, at Paris, the other day, which well
illustrates how flattery should not be given.
He was preaching before the king and his
ministers, and his subject was the uncertainty of
human life. 'My brethren,' said he, carried
away by a burst of eloquence, 'we must all
die!' Then, suddenly catching the king's eye,
he corrected himself, with a low bow to the
royal box—'Very nearly all of us, my brethren!'
I wonder if that was our good Beretti."

"He is incapable of such cowardice!" exclaimed Marie, firing up.

"Ho, ho, my daughter! lies the wind in that
quarter? Shall I tell you, now, what document
I found in the father's chamber? See here!"

The abbé pulled from his pocket the letter
which Beretti had cast aside after reading, to
wit—the notice to prisoner Dubourg that he had
been left a considerable fortune. "Now, why
is this letter left in a corner of the room, as if it
were waste paper. Has the poor prisoner been
advertised of his good fortune?"

One of the sisters was sent to invite the
governor of the fortress to wait upon the
abbé; and when that stout cavalier appeared,
he assured his hearers that it would be useless
to attempt to communicate with the prisoner,
but if the ladies would like to see him, and try
to explain the news, he would conduct them
to the iron cage with all the pleasure in the
world.

"Prisoners! iron cage!" murmured Ethel.
"This is the first time I have heard of them;
poor things, I should like to see how they
fare."

"It is not a place for ladies, but since mademoiselle wishes it——" said the governor.

"Let us all go!" said Sister Gabrielle, rising.

Accordingly torches were ordered, and the
party descended by stone staircases to the
dungeons, which were cut out of the rock.
Ethel and Marie had never been here before,
and the knowledge that such places existed
had been kept from them hitherto. Pausing
before an iron door, the governor stooped and
unlocked it, and one by one in the torch-lit
darkness they groped their way into a narrow
chamber. It was empty, but a wooden cage in
the further corner was discovered, in which

were some extremely narrow slits which let in
air to the person inside. This cage was also
opened, and immediately all thrust their sleeves
into their mouths and stopped their noses; two
torches were introduced, and revealed a hideous
spectacle.

A human creature without hair, teeth, or eyebrows, sat huddled up, blinking his eyes and
shivering with cold and ague. The floor of
his cage was reeking with damp and filth, and
his lower limbs had been paralyzed with wet
and cold; his toes had been gnawed by the
rats, and presented a row of red and putrid
stumps. When the governor said to him,
" Dubourg, you have had a fortune left you,"
the poor wretch opened his mouth and grinned
idiotically.

"Oh, come away!" cried Marie, half-dis-
gusted and half-afraid.

"And pray, what evil hath he done?" asked
Ethel, rather fiercely.

"C'est Dubourg, mademoiselle, gazetier de
Francfort. He wrote some articles injurious
to his Majesty, Le Grand Monarque," said the
governor.

"Le Grand Monarque," said Ethel in a tone
of contempt.

"And when will he forth again?" asked
Marie.

"When he dies, madame, and I care not how
soon. It is an ill office being warder to such
cattle; I like it not. Yet duty must be done."

That night the poor journalist of Frankfort
was remembered in the prayers of the three
women who had visited his prison. The abbé,
too, would perhaps have prayed for him, for he
had a kind heart; but the fact is, he sat up till
a late hour writing Greek sapphics, and quite
forgot to say his prayers at all: a dead loss to
the journalist of Frankfort.

But henceforth the grim grey walls and but-
tressed battlements of Mont St. Michel seemed
to grow less lovely to Marie and Ethel. In
vain the golden image of the archangel flashed
from the topmost pinnacle with upraised sword,
turning to meet the wind on his golden pivot.
He who had before seemed the protector of the
weak now appeared as a cruel gaoler. In the
heart of that rock, and under the very altar
of the God of Love, unavailing sighs and groans
were ascending from the victims of human
jealousy. The shadow that flung itself on the
sands seemed a type of the dark spirit that
haunted the abbey; and true was the legend

which told how the marvellous pile of buildings
was the creation of Satan. Was it a girlish
weakness which made them hurry through the
empty crypt and echoing cloister after dark,
making the torch flare and gutter and leave a
stream of blue smoke in their wake? Was it
a silly superstition which led them to people
the dripping catacombs with the spirits of mur-
dered men, and caused them to hear unearthly
sounds borne on the winds that shook their
window and howled amongst the grinning gar-
goyles? If so, they had a better excuse for
their fears and superstition, living as they did
in an age which believed in witches and ghosts
and second sight, than we have, who evoke
spirits from the vasty deep of a darkened
drawing-room, and converse with the souls of
dead men made perfect through the knuckles of
a professional juggler.

A few days after the visit to the dungeons,
when the sea was softly lapping about the foot
of the rock, and the myriad, unnumbered
dimples were smiling in the early autumn sun,
Gustave brought the fishing-boat alongside the
steps by the gate-way, and there stepped into
it Ethel and Marie and the abbé, and, not without remonstrance, Aunt Justine and her copy

of the " Law," as she named the Bible.   It was
the first time she had been prevailed upon to
dare the bosom of the deep, and the abbé was
in the mood to play upon her fears.

" See, madame, how the ocean, like a fawn-
ing greyhound, cringes before La Merveille,
and licks, as it were, the feet of our grand,
imperious abbey! Yet were but a little breath
to blow from the west, and you would see this
vile cockle-shell tossed upon a dangerous surf,
and France might mourn a bishop-designate,
Calvin a staunch misbeliever."

" A truce to your gibes, monseigneur; 'tis
unseemly to tempt Providence at any time ; how
much more so in so frail a boat as this! Not
that I fear for my own poor life, for He who
holds the waters in the hollow of His hand will
not suffer one of His elect to perish, unless,
indeed, He hath so designed it from His
counsels of eternity. Yet, I prythee, good
master Gustave, keep a good look-out for
whales, or any such Leviathan or Behemoth
that may chance to come our way.   There be
some beasts that have been delivered over to
Satan."

" Then, madame, I gather that your trust in
Providence is tempered by common sense.   It

varies inversely with the need of help; and in
a good, safe craft it would rise to a sense of
perfect security—n'est-ce pas ?"

"I decline to answer any suggestions to
infidelity," replied Aunt Justine, pursing up her
lips, and turning to the first chapter of Job with
so severe an air of concentration that the abbé
desisted from teazing her any more.

The boat's head was put out to sea, and the
abbé, taking off his domino and cassock, and
pushing his crystal spectacles up across his
forehead, settled down to the oar with a will,
glancing now and then to the stern of the boat,
if haply he might see Ethel and Marie rapt in
admiration of his skill and prowess. For the
good abbé was quite as proud of what he could
not do as of what he could, and he affected an
acquaintance with field-sports and gymnastic
exercises beyond what was thought creditable
to his cloth.

They had rowed out beyond the bay, and a
long reach of coast was visible on either side,
broken by headlands and bluff cliffs, while the
archangel seemed to have joined the mainland,
and the white houses of Avranches on the hill
had lessened to a shimmer of sunshine. All at
once Aunt Justine, who was bent on assisting

Providence by a diligent outlook, exclaimed—
"Here comes some monster! prenez-garde!"

From the northern headland a galley was
advancing with steady sweep of its long oars.

"Lay by, Gustave, we will await her here."

In a few minutes the red jackets of the
galley-slaves became visible, as they rose and
fell to the heavy oar, and shortly after the clank
of their chains was heard, and the sharp crack
of the comite's whip, as it descended on some
bare and quivering back.

"What think you, my daughters? shall we
go on board? 'Tis not so fearful a sight as you
may suppose. The poor men have their own
chaplain and everything they want, except
liberty," said Abbé Huet.

"Yes, you may chain their bodies, but you
cannot chain their mind. Hark!" cried Aunt
Justine.

The Huguenots were singing one of their
hymns as they rowed, and the rattle of their
clanking chains was the fierce accompaniment
to a wild but pathetic dirge. She was near
enough now for them to discern the name
painted gaudily on her bows, *L'Hirondelle*.
The abbé hailed them, gave his name and style,
and begged to be allowed to go on board.

At once the order was given to stop, and the captain of the galley stood hat in hand as the ladies stepped into his cabin. The two girls exchanged no words; to Marie it was like visiting some holy place, sanctified by the memory of a loved one departed. Ethel knew what was passing in her mind, and forbore to interrupt. The bland courtesies of the captain seemed as much out of place as the pestilent attentions of our modern vergers. Cakes and wine of Bordeaux were pressed upon the visitors, and some of the galley-slaves without played on musical instruments. As the abbé had sat down to a long chat and his third glass, and Aunt Justine was burning with eagerness to see the martyrs and confessors of her faith, the ladies accepted the escort of the chaplain to view the rest of the galley. The abbé remained in the cabin with the captain.

Amongst other remarks, the talk between these two presently fell upon the character and quality of the prisoners on board, and, amongst other galley-slaves, the captain mentioned a gentleman of noble birth, a Huguenot, who had lately been drafted into his vessel as a dangerous and lawless rebel. He had been put into an office of trust on board one of the other galleys,

and had been convicted on the evidence of two
of his fellow-prisoners of having stolen money
from the captain's locker to supply his co-
religionists with seditious books. "Accordingly," said the captain, "I have had him
placed in one of the hardest places in the galley
—but I am bound to say he behaves well, so
far."

"Ha! What is the name of this noble thief,
Monsieur le Capitaine ?"

"The Sieur de Cornelli," said the captain,
tossing off a glass of Bordeaux.

"Holy Virgin! Sieur de Cornelli! By my
soul, monsieur, an old friend of mine!—quite
incapable of doing what you accuse him of, I
swear to you. I would answer for his innocence with my life. Oh ciel! they will see
him. Ah! mon Dieu! that demoiselle is his
only daughter. I would not she found him for
a thousand livres. Oh! mon Dieu! mon
Dieu!"

The abbé ran out of the cabin and down the
coursier; but he was too late. The Lazarist
had not failed to call attention to the distinguished Huguenot, whom even bishops and
magistrates at St. Malo had visited the galley
on purpose to see; and De Cornelli, raising his

eyes and meeting his daughter's gaze, had made
a sudden gesture of surprise ; like a wounded
roe she had leapt into the bosom of her father,
sobbing, kissing, hugging, and thoroughly un-
manning him with emotion. The other galley-
slaves caught the infection of this tender sorrow,
and began to wipe their eyes with the backs of
their hands, while the comite and the argousin
and the Turk stood dumb with surprise.

When the little abbé ran down the *coursier*,
he saw mademoiselle clinging to her father's
neck, now commiserating him, and now pleading to the officers of the galley to release
him from his bench. It was a piteous sight
enough, and the abbé wrung his hands and
stamped and swore in two dead languages.

"What is to do ?" asked the captain, shrug-
ging his shoulders.

"Mon Dieu! je ne sais pas, moi!" cried
Huet.

But the sieur himself put an end to the
scene by pushing Marie gently from him ; but
ere he did so, he had squeezed something in
her hand. She knew not what, but held it tight
and kept it concealed. And then, after the
captain had ordered the argousin to take off his
chains, and had promised to treat him kindly

and make him store-keeper, they prevailed upon Marie to accompany them to the fishing-boat. Then, as she sank into her seat, she faintly heard the clank of the chains and the rush of the foaming wave, and faint and blurred before her tearful eyes the image of the gilded galley swam and faded. When she recovered from her long swoon, Ethel was sitting by her bed-side, weeping.

" I have been dreaming, Ethel ; I thought I had rescued my dear, dear father." And again, after a pause, " I have been selfish of late, ma chère ; I have thought only of my own welfare. I wish to live a new life. I will no longer envy you your great happiness. You deserve to be happy. I shall try and release my father ; it is my first duty."

Ethel understood not her words ; was she not wandering ? Poor child ! at last she sleeps.

CHAPTER XIII.

THE little crumpled piece of paper lay under
Marie's pillow that night, and long before the
angelus sounded in the morning, it had been
taken out, read, and re-read by the light of
a taper, while Ethel slept the sleep of the
weary.

Let us look over the shoulder of the galley-
slave's daughter, as she sits with her long brown
hair heaped about her shoulders.

" This, the fifth letter I send my sweet child,
I write not without pain. Oh! why dost thou
never answer? Do they keep my letters from
thee? It is another drop of bitterness in our
cup; may God stay me in His abundant love!
My darling—my Marie—I know thou hast not
forgotten me! I know thou hast not ceased to
love me because I suffer for opposing the
religion in which, by my consent, thou hast been

trained! No, I love to think, when in the cold
clear nights I gaze at the trembling stars, that
one day, very soon, I shall be united again to
my pure wife and our children.

"Since I last wrote I have changed my
galley, not altogether for the better; but I will
not trouble thee with my little sorrows, which
the good Father sends to make me hug closer
unto Him. The chaplain of this galley is a good
and kind Christian; we often argue together,
and he has lent me books by Bossuet and
others. I think he likes me because I dislike
Calvinists as well as Jesuits; he tells me I am
but half a heretic, and urges me to submit, to
the Church. But oh, Marie! I cannot do it,
though I should be restored to thee. I feel
now more than ever that God calls me to bear
witness against the spiritual oppression of this
deadly Church. Nay, what were it worth to
peril eternal life for a few short years of domestic peace! Oh, the lying and the cruelty of
many of these priests! And alas! amongst our
own confessors, what a dark picture of the merciful God hangs above the altar of their faith.

"Pray for me, sweet daughter, that I faint
not in obeying the call of conscience; pray, an
you will, that my conscience may be enlightened

to guide me to the truth; but oh that I may have strength to do what God bids me think His will! One word more: a trusty friend tells me that I and some others are to go shortly to Paris and thence to Marseilles. Adieu!"

Wild thoughts of heroic rescue were running through Marie's brain, when Ethel awoke and found her sitting beside her, with the sieur's letter fiercely held to her heart. The meeting with her father had turned the current of her being from meditation to action; the love so long pent-up in her bosom began to seek an outlet in doing and daring something for her father's sake.

When the two girls entered the church of the abbey they were startled at first on seeing, instead of the usual half-dozen peasant women and three old sailors who commonly made up the congregation at matins, a motley group of strangers, who stared at them with wide eyes and gibbered at one another in the Breton dialect. The church, too, was gaily decorated with streamers and bannerets, and the priests wore new vestments in honour of their patron saint, whose feast it was that day.

After the short early service of matins, Marie and Ethel strolled out upon the *promenoir*, as the little terrace was called, which communicated with a side door of the church and commanded an extensive view over the *grève*, the distant hill of Avranches, and the creeping sea. Along the sands, by the road marked out by long poles planted at various angles to guide the stranger, they described numerous black figures dotting the grey desert. They were ecclesiastics, peasants, burghers, or, more frequently, the widows of men who had fallen in the wars of Le Grand Monarque, coming with their pious offerings to celebrate the fête of St. Michel and All Angels; coming not altogether without regard to St. Soi-Même, prepared to sacrifice something having an exchange value, and hoping to get their *quid pro quo*, substantially, in the healing of their sick folk at home, in the begetting of male offspring, in the miraculous payment of the gabelle or octroi, in the replenishing of ruined homesteads, and if not that, why at least spiritually, in the compensation for moral improvements which eternity and the Pope between them had to offer. And so the little town was beginning to fill with the pilgrims, and from their breezy height the two girls could hear the hum of many voices down amongst the townsfolk.

They had not long been gazing over the parapet towards the flat and dismal marshes of Pontorson, when the Abbé Huet came striding towards them in some haste.

" Eh! vous voilà encore!" he cried, touching Marie lightly on the elbow.

" Encore, monseigneur? I have not met you before this morning," said Marie.

" Parbleu! Je ne sais pas, ma fille. I would have taken an oath on the relics yonder that I saw you five minutes ago talking to Gustave; and what's more, the old fishwives have got it in their heads that you are a white witch!"

" À Dieu ne plaise, monseigneur," cried Marie, throwing up both her arms.

" Il est vrai pourtant; and the hide-bound humour of these marine goddesses can be guided by no feats of logic or *elenchus rationis;* I have argued, but still they persist that you are a white witch."

And very like a white witch looked Marie at that moment, as her dark hair tumbled in the wind across her blanched and terrified face, while the dark grey eyes turned from the abbé to Ethel, and again from Ethel to the abbé, as if to gather from their looks what they deemed her to be. It was no laughing matter to count

as a witch among those wild Breton Catholics,
whose blood had been newly stirred by tor-
turing the Huguenots.

They descended the winding staircase that
led to la Mère Gabrielle's apartments, from
which they could see the movements of the
crowd who thronged the little Cour du Lion
below and the ramparts of the walls. The kind
sweet-faced abbess smiled Marie's fears away,
and smoothed the dark hair from her brow with
soothing words.

"The poor unlettered denizens of the wil-
derness only mean to compliment thee, my
daughter. A white witch only does deeds of
loving-kindness, though in marvellous ways,
they say. She would not hurt a soul; therefore
assure thyself that no evil will befall thee from
the pilgrims, who would not for their own sake
harm a white witch."

So Marie grew calmer, and almost forgot her
alarm in watching the pilgrims as they passed
along the rampart to the abbey church. When
the time came for celebrating the second service, Marie, as usual, attended Sister Gabrielle
to the enclosed portion of the church, where the
old nuns were wont to pray or nod in seclusion,
but Ethel obtained permission, as being a

heretic, to mingle with the main body of wor-
shippers in the nave of the church.

It was indeed a strange spectacle to behold,
when, at the tinkling of the bell, that motley
crowd, drawn from sea and shore and distant
country towns, sank low upon bended knee,
while the clouds of incense seemed to veil with
mysterious secrecy the presence of God within
the Host; and Ethel, with closed eyes and bent
head, was rapt in meditation such as the solemn
moment inspired her, when she felt that some-
one at her side was pulling her dress—not once,
as if by accident, but in successive jerks. She
looked round reprovingly at a young peasant-
girl who knelt by her side, and whose face was
concealed, as she knelt forward, by the large
bonnet of her class ; but what was her astonishment to recognize Marie in the suddenly up-
lifted face ! Ethel almost uttered a cry of
surprise, and a thrill passed through her, making
her knees tremble beneath her. Surely Satan
was using Marie's image for his own dark
purpose! But the white witch, or whatever
she was, put her finger to her lips, as if to
demand secrecy. It was no peasant's hand—
the fingers finely tapering, the nails delicately
kept.

Ethel, fascinated by the face, could not take
her eyes off for an instant; and though it was
only for a few seconds, she seemed to be
perusing that clear, milk-white complexion,
those dark, arching eyebrows, that full pink,
envermeiled lip, for an age.   It was Marie, and
yet it was not Marie.   One moment she shivered
with awe, the next a confused remembrance of
a face seen before agitated her mind.   At last,
she spelt out the mystery when, as the worship-
pers bent lower, a pair of blue eyes laughed
softly in the old familiar manner of Philippe.
Two feelings then struggled for the mastery in
Ethel's breast—joy and alarm; joy that the
white witch was a friend disguised, alarm for
his safely in the midst of an excited throng of
bigots.

It was not until the voices of the choir were
raised in the chaunt that Philippe dared to say
anything to Ethel; he then whispered—

"Henri and I are staying with Gustave;
contrive to meet me this afternoon on Tombelaine."

Ethel inclined her head in token of assent,
and immediately the peasant-girl was gone, and
she was left alone amongst the dark-eyed
Bretons.   How she hungered for the service to

conclude ; how she longed to meet Marie and tell her the news ! But as ill luck would have it, when Marie at length came from the church, the abbess was with her, and by no secret sign could Ethel get her friend to understand that she wished her to retire to her own room. And then the abbé came up, insisting that his daughters, as he called them, should come and see the provisions carried up the tunnel on the face of La Merveille. So they repaired to the *salle des gardes*, near which was the great wheel and the rope by means of which the garrison formerly used to draw up what was required; but to-day, in consequence of the influx of strangers, this custom, which had remained for some time in abeyance, was to be renewed.

As they stepped to the edge of the platform of rock and gazed into the sheer abyss below them, where nestled the tiny homes of the Montois, creeping like startled chicks under the shadow of their mother's wing, the hum of voices suddenly broke out into a yell of fury or alarm.

"Eh, ma foi !" cried the abbé ; "the vulgus profanum are abroad ; sæviunt gentes !"

Ethel held on by Marie's skirt and peered

over the dizzy precipice. Marie, not aware that
her interests were at all involved in such vulgar
commotion, folded her arms across her breast
and flew on the wings of fancy to *L'Hirondelle*.
There, as she was delivering her father from
the chains of the galley and receiving the meed
of her labours in the embraces of him whom
she had ransomed, a sudden twitch of her robe,
a sharp clasping of her arm by Ethel's fingers,
dispelled the dream, and startled her again into
the inevitable present.

"Qu'est-ce qu'il y a ?"

"Regardez !"

The two girls bent over the edge of the rock,
the abbé remonstrating in vain, and holding on
to Marie's dress from a secure position in the
rear. The shouts of the crowd below, which
had ceased for a few moments, had now re-
doubled; heads appeared mounting the steps
leading to the battlements. The flutter of a
girl's petticoats was seen a few paces in front;
presently, as she came round an angle in the
wall, she was seen to be running at full speed,
pursued by half a dozen yelling savages, whose
goat-skin coverings floated behind them in the
wind. The girl, however, gained on her pursuers, until a sentinel started from his box

on the walls and planted himself full in her
way.

"Oh! Marie!" exclaimed Ethel, in an agony
of suspense.

"Comment! it is only a thief, perhaps; she
has been stealing, doubtless."

Ethel dare not tell her suspicions, lest the
abbé should hear. Meanwhile the sentinel,
instead of stopping the girl, had stepped aside
and made the sign of the cross and spat three
times.

But the Bretons had profited by the check
which the sentinel had given the fugitive to
come close to her heels, and as they raced up
the stone steps—for the wall in this place was
carried at a steep incline up the rock—the clatter
of their *sabots* was heard distinctly in the *salle
des gardes* above. The wall and the promenade
upon it ended at a few paces beyond in the
vertical face of the cliff, and it seemed that a
capture was imminent. But the girl bounded
like a wild goat over the parapet, and alighted
fully seven feet below upon the loose stones
which had crumbled from the cliff. Her pursuers stood for a moment looking over the
wall, and not caring to risk the fracture of a
limb, but when one of them discovered an

easier place higher up, they followed her in full
cry over the *débris* and crumbling rock.

Ethel and Marie lost sight of the girl for
a few moments, as she was immediately beneath
where they were standing, but soon a slender
hand appeared clutching the platform of rock
which served as the base of the tunnel or
tramway on to which the provision basket
was lowered. Slowly and with difficulty she
mounted upon the ledge of rock, gave one look
up at the precipitous cliff which frowned above,
and was about to run down on the other side
by the foot-path which led direct into the town,
when a voice from above arrested her.

"Montez, montez sur la cage!"

The girl looked up at the dark, cavernous
hole which yawned in the masonry of La
Merveille, and descried two figures leaning towards her with outstretched hands. Already
the fingers of her pursuers were clutching the
edge of the rock on which she stood. There
was no time for consideration. To run down
into the narrow street was to run into the lion's
jaws. She jumped into the cage, making the
rope vibrate, and sending a shiver to the heart
of the great wheel, and tightening the coils
that were already circling the dusty windlass.

Ethel rushed to the wheel, calling to her
companions to help, and by their united efforts
the spokes moved round, the windlass creaked,
the rope grew thicker in its bed. Ethel worked
till the veins started out of her forehead and
her fore-arm ached ; the abbé, thrusting aside
his *soutane*, put forth the strength of a gymnast,
if only to manifest his prowess ; Marie put her
left hand delicately to the handle, and contem-
plated the exertions of her companions with an
air of amusement—not that she was devoid of
sympathy for the poor hunted creature, but
because her experience of Breton character had
induced in her a tendency to side with the
policeman, whether official or amateur, as the
gentlemen who stood howling below appeared
to be ; and on the present occasion she could
not help being somewhat amused at the en-
thusiasm displayed by Ethel and paraded by
monseigneur in the cause of a young person
whose conduct, she doubted not, would prove
to have been as light as her fingers.

But in a moment the chamber was darkened
by the cage, and its occupant, stepping lightly
forth, stood irresolute, unable to adjust a bewildered vision to the sudden change from sunshine to gloom.

"The white witch!" ejaculated the abbé, unconsciously retiring two steps.

"Marie!" cried Ethel, in a tone of suppressed delight, "c'est lui!"

"Who? What is it?"

The boy rushed forward and threw his arms about his sister's neck.

"Dost thou not know me, then?" he exclaimed, holding her at arms' length, and again pressing his lips against her cheek.

Meanwhile the abbé, half-angry and half-puzzled, had approached Ethel and inquired who the counterfeit maiden really was; but when he learned that the tall, fair-faced boy was the little Philippe of olden memories, he ran to him and kissed him on both cheeks twice over.

"But we must conceal the lad, Marie, before any one finds him here."

"True, monseigneur; where shall we place him?"

"In my chamber; yours would not be safe, for they might search it to find the white witch. By the way, Phil, why were those men after you?"

"You have guessed it, mon père. They took me for a witch, and would have drowned me

had I not tucked up my petticoats to good
purpose."

"Hé bien, mon fils! go with thy sister while
I stay here to cover thy retreat. They shall
not hurt a hair of thy head. I am no advocate,
myself, of haling men into the bosom of Holy
Church by the throat."

Marie and Philippe hastened away; the abbé
turned to Ethel and said—

"Speak now, ma fille; how think you I have
behaved in this business?"

"I see now," said Ethel archly, "that your
reverence possesseth second sight."

CHAPTER XIV.

"AND now tell me all about yourself, mon frère," said Marie, when she had given Philippe a cordial and washed the dirt from his face and hands. And her heart beat faster; out of curiosity, no doubt, for she had surrendered the idol whom her heart now almost despised.

The boy sat with his arm round his sister's neck. You would have sworn they were two sisters, so delicate was the tint on his cheek, so white his neck and arms, which were somewhat exposed by the dress he now wore.

"We have been here, now, some days, Marie, waiting for the chance of getting speech with you. Gustave is a faithful friend, and supplies us with lodging and food, as you know, doubtless. Strange! after all our travels in search of our dear father, where we could learn no tidings of

him, to come here with the intention of communicating to you our fruitless search, and find
here the traces which we so much desired!
Gustave told us about your meeting with him
in the galley, and since then Henri has had a
letter from St. Malo, requesting that you and
Ethel will go south into the Cevennes, where
we have some relations who are willing to take
care of you for a time. That is what I wanted
to tell you."

"Oh Philippe! into the Cevennes! Hélas!
that would be even worse than to be confined
in the prison of St. Michel! I have heard of
horrible scenes enacted in those forbidding
mountains, where the Calvinists are furious
fanatics and slaughter all good Catholics."

"Fi donc, ma sœur! You have heard a
garbled account of those brave mountaineers
from persons who are prejudiced. They have
hearts as soft as women's, but they are brave as
lions, and proud, too! I hear they will brook no
interference of priest or king between their con-
sciences and their God—but I forget. I am
talking to a Catholic; my sister is on the side
of those who persecute her father, as they
persecuted even unto death her mother and the
little angel-babe.'

"Oh Philippe!" sobbed Marie, throwing her-self passionately on his neck, while the boy, whose cheek was flaming with indignant emotion, bent over her tenderly and soothed her with soft caresses.

After the storm of sobs had subsided, Marie lifted her head and shook the wayward tresses back from her flushed face, and murmured—

" I shall live and die a good Catholic, I hope and pray; but never, dear Phil, can I look upon my sweet father as aught but a martyr; and I think our good Bishop of Coutances would agree with me in this. Let us not argue about doctrines. God knoweth how you and I and our poor father are knit together in love; God will see resemblances in our several loves for Him, where we mark only differences. Man makes the heretic, God maketh the saint. I doubt not I shall meet in the heavenly home many whom we Catholics have cast out as lost. The bosom of our merciful Lord is wider than the arms of St. Peter."

" Thou art a good girl. Would that all Catholics thought with thee, then were there no heretics in the world, Marie. And thou wilt come with Henri and me into the Cevennes·? Nay! it will be but following our father thither, since he goes to Marseilles shortly. And who knows? perhaps, as Henri says, we shall find some means of rescuing him as he passes with the chain through that turbulent and warlike race of men!"

There was a cloud settling on Marie's brow. At length she spoke—

"It were a noble enterprise to adventure life for one's father. But how can we, who are both young girls, travel through France with you and Henri? Who is to protect us? Mon frère, we had far better stay here!"

"Pas du tout! Henri has thought it all out with his usual wisdom. Ah! there is a true friend indeed!—and I know not how it is, Marie, that thou hast treated him with scant courtesy of late. If thou hadst heard, as I have, how he admires thy piety and patience, thou wouldst——"

"Tush, Philippe! let us talk on other subjects. I am much obliged to Monsieur Guillot for his high regard for my unworthy self, still more for his constant care of thee. But he doubtless has his motives;—young men usually have strong motives when they are so seemingly unselfish."

The boy looked blankly in his sister's face,

and wondered what the riddle was which had
so mystified the tale of girlish love. However,
he resumed, with a sigh expressive of regret for
broken confidences—

"Mais, enfin! we must decide quickly this
way or that, for Henri and I dare not stay
long in St. Michel, now suspicion has been
awakened. His plan was that I should accompany you and Ethel on board the frigate which
lies yonder in the offing, and will take us to
Narbonne, or some other landing-place near the
mouth of the Rhone. There our cousins will
meet us and convey us safely to their home in
the mountains."

" Those cousins—we know them not—can we
trust them ?"

" My father recommends the plan, and that is
enough for me. And whilst we sail southwards,
Henri has promised to follow close on the steps
of our dear father, so that there may be no
chance of losing him again."

"It is well schemed, mon frère. I will acquaint
Ethel with your plan, and you and Gustave
shall arrange our escape from this abbey-
fortress."

At this moment the door opened, and
Philippe rose from his chair as the abbé entered

the chamber, bearing in his hands a flagon of
wine. Behind him came Ethel, laden with a
bowl of steaming *potage*, in which floated sweet
herbs and sops of new bread.

"Allons! eat while you may, my young
friend; carpe diem! 'Either take thy liquor or
thy leave,' as the Greek proverb saith. Ha, ha!
'twas a merry jest that we—mademoiselle et
moi—had to play in thy absence. Such a ham-
mering at the gates! such a babel of garlic-
scented voices! such a crying out for the white
witch, I never before heard! They would
hardly be appeased when I went out and
lectured them on the impropriety of hunting to
death a creature which only plays good pranks
among mortals. A baby had had a fit, they
said, when she passed, and a cat had eaten up
her kittens under the influence of her shadow.
Çependant, mes filles, I promised to exorcise
her with the spell of Johannes Magicus, and a
few *deniers* amongst the noisiest sent them back
happily to the cider merchants, where they are
now drinking to the white witch of the house
of De Cornelli."

"Then here's to the health of monseigneur!"
said Philippe, tossing off his glass.

"And now may we not hear what you have

been doing all this time, and whither you have travelled ? " said Ethel, when the boy had finished his soup.

" Have you not heard it from Monsieur Henri already ? " asked Marie, with a touch of scorn in her manner that did not escape Ethel.

" How should I ? " replied the girl, colouring with vexation, and adding thereby one more piece of cumulative evidence to the little heap of proof which Marie was gathering in, that she might make a bonfire of her girlish love and early friendship, and start anew in sackcloth and ashes—ashes internal as well as external, if God so willed it.

" Perhaps," said Philippe, " I shall compromise monseigneur if I tell him all, and inform him where my companions now are. He may feel himself bound to communicate the news to his superiors."

" Pas du tout, mon cher, pas du tout ! " cried the little abbé, energetically rising from his *fauteuil* and letting himself drop with an elastic abandon into the cushioned seat. " Say what you like, and never fear that I shall make use of your statements. There is a time to confess and a time to hold one's peace ; commencez donc, mon cher fils."

"Well, to begin at the beginning, I must tell you that we landed from the Dutch frigate near Havre, and took a boat up the Seine till we came to Caudebec. There we bought a little cart, to which we harnessed Maintenon, much against his will, and started by the road to Rouen. The spring flowers were coming out, and the river banks were fragrant with the white apple-blossom. But the miserable condition of the peasantry whom we met roused Henri's indignation so fiercely against his majesty the king, that we were nearly arrested on suspicion of being foreign spies, especially as Henri kept quoting some English he had learned from mademoiselle. I heard him say it so often that the words stay with me still: 'It is pleasant travelling when you are guarded by poverty and guided by love.'"

"Très bien! who saith that among your writers, my daughter?"

"I think it is Sir Walter Raleigh, monseigneur," replied Ethel.

"So she loved him even then!" thought Marie, silencing a deep sigh.

"And so at last to Rouen, where we lay at the White Cross inn one night; called next day at the gaol, and found that two chains

had just started, one for Paris and the other for
St. Malo. The gaoler bade us hasten to Paris,
where he said we should probably find the
Sieur de Cornelli in the 'Tournelle,' *en route*
for Marseilles.

"So we started for Paris, habited like travelling merchants, and much ado we had at first to
make Maintenon sustain his character with due
regard to propriety. More than once he bolted
after a wild rabbit and overturned the cart in
which our merchandise was supposed to lie. In
some towns through which we passed, the
persecution was still going on. Soldiers were
living at free quarters, throwing valuable furniture out of window, insulting delicate women by
exposing them in the public streets in a half-
naked state. In one street through which we
passed, a lady had just given birth to an infant
on her own doorstep, whilst the dragoons inside
were smoking and drinking in her bed-room.
We found it difficult in times like those to
restrain our indignation and assume an air of
indifference, but we were so closely watched
that the least imprudence would have cost us
our liberty.

"Ah! it was a weary time, trudging along
the dusty roads without stopping to look down

at the winding Seine or pluck a blue-bell in the
neighbouring woods! And so at last we saw
the spires and tall chimneys of Paris beyond
us, and my heart began to beat quick with the
hope of once more beholding my father. But
oh! the smell of the streets to one used to our
sweet Normandy! It was as if sulphur had been
mixed with mud. We lay at the Ville de
Venice that night, and the next morning we
passed from the town to the city, which you
knows lies between the former and the
university, in form of an island. As we passed
over the Pont Neuf, we paused to gaze awhile
on the curious medley of passers-by; for there
is one large passage for coaches and two for foot
passengers, three or four feet higher. And on
the middle of the bridge stands the famous
statue of Henri le Grand on horseback, by John
di Bologna. There is an iron grate about the
statue, and here a great crowd of idlers was
collected to view the feats of the mountebanks.
We were attracted in particular by some
marionnettes, with which there was performing
a monkey, who was dressed like a dragoon, and
who amused the populace by firing off a musket
at a stuffed figure in a white shirt, labelled
'Camisard' on his back. Henri asked a little

sallow-faced man who stood by us the meaning
of this 'Camisard.'

"'Morbleu!' ejaculated the fellow, 'are you
then from the provinces? A Camisard is a
heretic; he lives in Languedoc, or about there,
and cuts the throats of any priests he can catch.
"Enfants de Dieu," they call themselves.
"Enfants du Diable," rather! Vive le Roi! he
has drawn the sword from the scabbard at
last.'

"At this moment there was a movement
in the crowd, and several hats were raised as a
brilliantly appointed coach came rumbling over
the bridge. There were outriders on either
side richly liveried, in black velvet *toques* and
scarlet coloured *justaucorps*. Inside the coach
sat a graceful but contemptuous-looking gentleman, habited in a suit so covered with rich
embroidery that one could perceive nothing of
the stuff under it. He had a page by his side,
who kept taking off his hat and waving the long
red feather out of the window to save his master
the trouble of returning the salutes of the
mob.

"'Voilà monsieur, le Comte de Lauzun!'
said our sallow friend. 'He goes to the gaming-
table, the only amusement left him now that he

is banished from the court. They say he is prouder than his majesty himself.'

" Just then two archers of the guard came up and arrested us in the king's name, to our great amazement; for we did not know what offence we had committed. But from the fact that our sallow friend was manacled and we were not, we concluded that he was the culprit, and we were arrested as being seen in his company. And so it turned out; for on arriving at the *châtelet* or prison, we were interrogated as to our knowledge of the fellow, and, on our explaining the circumstances, were allowed to stand down while he was put to the question; Maintenon and his little cart remaining without in charge of the porter.

" It seems he was suspected of a robbery, and not choosing to confess, or perhaps being inno-cent, was by the lieutenant put to the torture. You may think we did not feel very comfort-able, fearing lest in his agony he should even implicate us. They first bound his wrist with a strong rope, and one end of it to an iron ring made fast to the wall about four feet from the floor, and then his feet with another cable, fastened about five feet further than his utmost length to another ring on the floor of the room.

When he was thus suspended, and yet lying but aslant, they slid a horse of wood under the rope which bound his feet, which so exceedingly stiffened it, as severed the fellow's joints in miserable sort, drawing him out at length in an extraordinary manner. But when he still confessed nothing, the executioner, with a horn (just such as they drench horses with), stuck the end of it into his mouth, and poured the quantity of two buckets of water down his throat and over him, which so prodigiously swelled him, as would have pitied and affrighted any one to see it. They then let him down, and carried him before a warm fire to bring him to himself, being now to all appearance dead with pain.

"'Eh bien, monsieur!' said the lieutenant to him, as he lay unconscious, 'we cannot hang you, but you shall away to the galleys, for the evidence is against you.'

"And so we were dismissed, wondering silently, if that was justice, what injustice should be like! At the door of the *châtelet* stood the porter, waiting to tell us that a man had just passed, and had asked of him who owned the dog, and what manner of men they were who owned it. 'And when I told him, sirs, he bade me say he would meet you outside the Hôtel-Dieu, close to Notre-Dame, where he had business immediate.'

"'Nay, sir,' replied Henri, 'we have had enough of casual acquaintances for one day! Who knows that this fellow may not hail us to the torture?'

"'Ma foi! the hound seemed to know him as an old friend, for he nearly overturned his cart, jumping up to caress him, barking, wagging his tail. I thought we should have the provost out to see what was toward!'

"On hearing this, as you may conjecture, we hurried away to the Hôtel-Dieu, wondering vastly who this old friend should be whom Maintenon so warmly welcomed; for it was impossible to think the hound could either be mistaken, or make a light acquaintance with a stranger, seeing that he loves not new faces. Mais enfin! when we came to the door of this great pile of buildings, we could nowhere see the man we wanted, and were amazed at the number of people who were hurrying in and out, some with fresh patients, as the word is, and some with puckered chins, as though they were about to face a miserable spectacle. Then one stood and beckoned us into the hospital,

saying that he had been commissioned by one
within to conduct such as we to the children's
ward. And so, leaving Maintenon with the
porter, we followed our guide between rows of
beds occupied by sick folk in various stages of
disease, and there, bending over the pallets with
their phials, or sponges, stood the daughters
of St. Vincent de Paul, while stout and self-
important chirurgeons, in their square caps and
long black gowns, strutted to and fro, giving
their orders and administering here a bolus
and there an emetic. It was a strange sight,
yet I could not help thinking that if it were not
for the intolerable stench these unhappy creatures would be content enough; and Henri said
it was wondrous how clean and orderly all was,
compared with the loathsome hospitals in the
provinces.

"After winding in and out through several
chambers, we came at last into a long apartment
whose little beds betokened the use to which
it was put.

"'Voilà monsieur, qui vous cherche!' said
our guide; and who should come to meet us
but Durand, the stonemason, the tears in his
eyes, and his forehead all red and swollen.

"'La petite — Jeannette — elle meurt — je

n'avons espoir,' he stammered out in his broken *batois;* then pointed to the little pallet-bed.

"A sister of charity knelt beside the child, holding the crucifix before her eyes. Jeannette, wasted to her shadow, lay breathing short, her large bright eyes fixed on the crucifix.

"'She cannot see you now—she is almost in heaven,' murmured Durand. But the child's lips moved; we all bent over her.

"'I can see her now, the Lady of Coutances. She wears the little wreath of blue-bells and primroses which I wove for her; but she looks so sad. Ah! I forgot! they killed her son, the sweet, good Jesus; yes, madame, I am coming as fast as I can. Au! quel plaisir! The Lady de Cornelli too! Yes, madame, they killed you, too; but all will be well at last. Nay, madame, I protest I know not if the good Lord Christ were a Catholic or no; my father is not, and he loves your son, madame. They have tried to make me hate my father, madame, but he has come to see me at last, poor man! and if I love not my father, how can I love the gentle Jesus, whom I only see in my dreams?' At this, the child's eyes fell on poor Durand's face. 'Mon père, do not weep for me. I shall soon be very happy. Thy little Jeannette is

going amongst kind friends. She will ask the
Mother of our Lord to let thee carve more
angel faces; then dear mother will be glad, and
Marguerite will be brave and bonny amongst
the school-girls—or say, father dear, wilt rather
come with me, and sculpture yet rarer faces in
the golden heaven? Come! oh, mon père!
for I may wait no longer—no longer——'

"We knelt, for the soul was winging her
upward flight to the unseen world.

"When Durand rose from his knees, he was
calmer; he said to Henri—

"'I could not have wished her a happier
death-bed; thanks to the good Abbé Huet, who
had the poor little thing removed from the foul
lazar-house in which she was rotting at Caen
to this public home. But come, messieurs, let
us step out into the street awhile!' And then
he told us how he had escaped from the chain
as he was going to the galleys, and had sought
Jeannette and found her at Paris."

The abbé had listened with glittering eyes to
Philippe's account of poor little Jeannette, for
whom at Caen he had contracted a real pity.
I say real, because this great scholar and
learned theologian did not usually take much
interest in any man, woman, or child, who met

his outward gaze as a living and visible suf-
ferer. To insure his sympathy, it was necessary
to approach him through the spirit, and not
through the senses ; through the imagination,
and not through the coarse medium of tym-
panum or retina. He would weep and suffer
sympathetically over any person whom he en-
visaged either from the portraiture of a book
or the working of his own fancy, but he would
readily walk a furlong to get quit of any
spectacle of real and present misery. In short,
he was capable of a vast amount of ideal
emotion, but the education which his mind had
undergone had unfitted him for the exercise of
a living sympathy.

Such characters are still to be met with, even
in this age of iron and steam ; and though it
seems a pity that a man should only be able
to compassionate the dead or the non-existing—
to exercise his emotion, in short, only when it is
too late to be of any service—yet a mind so
trained benefits mankind indirectly through the
medium of literature. Such a man will write so
as to stir up the emotions of others, and their
good works must in part be paid in to his
credit.

When, then, Philippe narrated the simple story

of Jeannette's death, the living child-sufferer of the filthy hospital at Caen was transformed into an ideal character. The abbé's senses were no longer jarred by unseemly sights and noisome smells; he could surrender himself to the luxury of pure contemplation; and in so doing he unconsciously drew the sleeve of his *soutane* across his eyes, for there was something there which dimmed those organs. And Marie looked at the abbé with rising admiration—"Then monseigneur has a heart, after all!" she thought to herself.

Philippe took another sip of the red wine, and continued his story—

"The next day Durand came to our lodging, and conducted us, as he had appointed, to the Château de la Tournelle, where he had learned that great many convicts and sufferers for the faith were confined. But I must tell you that before starting I was disguised in the dress of a grey sister, as none but they and the priests were admitted within the castle. Hé bien! when we arrived within the courtyard, I some paces in the rear, as having nothing in common with the other two, a new batch of convicts was on the point of departing, so you may imagine we eagerly scanned their faces, if haply our dear father's might be amongst them. And whilst Henri and Durand were so engaged, I profited by the confusion to slip in unobserved; but as I was unused to the place I failed to take the right turning, and came suddenly upon a fat Jesuit who was pacing the corridor, mass-book in hand. At first he looked angry at being disturbed, but when I apologized, saying I had missed my way in trying to reach the dungeons, he put his hand on my shoulder, spoke kindly, stroked my cheek, said I was very young and too pretty to come among such rough scoundrels, and insisted on accompanying me to the steps leading to the dungeons. I was glad to be free of him, I assure you, for my silly pink face mightily attracted his reverence!

"However, my amusement was speedily dispelled when I stepped into the gloomy vault in which the prisoners were confined. There were huge beams of oak placed at the distance of about three feet apart, and so arranged and fixed in some way to the floor, that at first sight one would take them for benches. But on approaching them, I saw they were used for a very different purpose. Thick iron chains were attached to these beams, one and a half feet in length, and two feet apart, and at the end of these chains was an iron collar, through which was thrust the neck of a convict. The beams seemed to be about forty feet long, and twenty men were chained to them in file. The chamber was round, and large enough to contain five hundred men. But the most dreadful part of all this was to behold the attitudes and postures of these wretches; for they could not lie down at full length, because the beam to which their necks were fixed was too high, neither could they sit or stand upright, the beam being too low; their attitude seemed to be half-lying, half-sitting, part of the body being upon the stones, the other part upon this beam.

" I found my way to the red jackets of our confessors, and set them to mutual inquiries amongst themselves for the Sieur de Cornelli. And it was easy enough to address them without being overheard by the grey sisters, who were going about with soup and bread, by reason of the constant noise of groans and mournful lamentations with which the dungeon echoed; though every now and then the turn-keys would enter, and with huge ox-bones strike barbarously on the heads and shoulders of old men whose limbs were racked with intolerable cramping pains, they told me. There were some men of culture and refinement amongst these *miserables*, as I gathered from the short conversation I had there ; but alas! not one had heard of our dear father.   They seemed to think he must be still on the northern sea-coast ; for one of the galley-slaves, whom the others jestingly called 'mother's favourite,' plucked the mother-superior by the sleeve, and asked her if she remembered De Cornelli, to which she replied, 'Non, malheureusement, non!' and then eyed me so curiously that I was glad to sneak out again."

Marie, who had hitherto listened with a pained expression, inquired—

"Is it possible, mon frère, that those unhappy men can jest amid their sufferings ?"

"Oh, certainement! many of the younger and stronger affected to make light of it.   Indeed, the air of gaiety observable in that den of anguish struck me as most heart-rending. Ethel knows our character now ; if anybody is gay on the day of doom, it will be a Frenchman!"

"Ridiculum ferient ruinæ!" murmured the abbé, smiling to himself.

"Well! on arriving outside I found Henri and Durand talking through the double-grating of the dungeon window to the prisoners. I had not noticed them when I was within; but it seems these were the favoured few who, on payment of fifty crowns, were allowed to be chained by the foot near the window with a chain two yards long."

"How horrible you are, Philippe, with your 'chains' and 'groans' and 'dark dungeons!' I protest, you fairly make my flesh creep!" said Marie.

"Nay, I would to God I could make thy heart-strings crack, and thy tears come to thine eyes, as they did to mine, when I thought of the cause for which many of these noble fellows were treated worse than dogs! If thou couldst see with thine own eyes what the priests do in the way of hounding on the cruel passions of the mob, thou wouldst waver, methinks, in thy allegiance to the Pope and his myrmidons."

"Eh, ma foi!" cried the abbé, taking off his spectacles and rubbing them up and down his sleeve; "this is rank heresy! this is your very pestilent heterodoxy! and in my presence, too! a bishop-elect! Young man, you are very ignorant; you have never studied the fathers. St. Chrysostôme and St. Jerome are sealed books; St. Augustine I dare say you never read

in your life; the schoolmen, the theologians of
the last century, all absolutely unknown! And
yet, monsieur, you dare to pass a flippant judgment on the wisdom of the old and new world
combined!"

"Pardon, Monsieur l'Abbé. I know nothing
of opinions, either old or new. I only infer that
the tree is corrupt if the fruit is corrupt; and
deferring in all matters of knowledge to your
reverence's great learning, I yet humbly think
that I am as able to distinguish good from evil
as the most deeply tinctured in the learning of
the ancients."

"Humph!" exclaimed Huet, a little mollified
by the boy's respectful bearing towards himself;
"much you know about good and evil! Why,
Plato held that sin was the consequence of
ignorance. I think so, too. I think that you,
in your ignorance, are very likely to mistake
evil for good, and good for evil."

"And I, monseigneur, think that you, with all
your learning, are very likely to acquiesce in
cruelties which you know to be wrong, because
your sympathies are not with the living but
with the dead!"

"Comment, rude boy! you shall repent this!"
cried the abbé, starting up.

But Marie clung to his arm, and looked up in so piteous a sort that he relinquished his first idea, which was to go straight to the governor and acquaint him with the name and condition of his visitor. Marie and Ethel prevailed upon him to resume his seat with some difficulty.

"It must be understood, then, that no loose rhetorical statements are to be made, Monsieur Philippe, tending to discredit your sister's religion."

"Oh, monseigneur," cried Marie, "nothing could shake my faith!"

"Vraiment!" said the abbé; "what! got beyond foundations on reason and authority, and suspended as it were by golden links from heaven!"

Marie blushed; she felt it was a compliment she hardly deserved.

"Ma foi! I never got so far as that myself; as a Christian, I am dependent on logic and the laws of thought. Boy, when you are older, you will know that heresy is a poison which must be grubbed up, rent, annihilated, or it will o'er-spread God's goodly garden."

"Aye, monseigneur; I read as much in my history of Greece, when I was told how Anax-agoras the philosopher and Socrates the reformer fared at the hands of gardeners who had a like fashion of cutting and pruning what they judged heresy."

"Le bon Dieu! Now Philippe, I forgive you for that argument; it is quite cheering to hear such names on the lips of youth. Yet I would have you know that there is no parallel to be drawn between those times of merely human wisdom and these present days. Voyez! then it was one man's wit against another's, where freedom of debate should have forwarded truth; but here it is Luther and Calvin and Erasmus against divine intelligence—human ignorance setting itself up against revelation, the Church! 'Twould be folly not to stamp out heresy, and more cruel in the end. And take my word for it, the Holy Church is compelled, on her very honour, to allow no schism from her body; and if ever a time does come when she shall seem to tolerate heresy, it will only be because she cannot see her way to annihilate her opponent. Give her time, give her power, and she will strangle the error she has permitted to play child-like about her knees!"

Ethel looked up and said, "We have got a great way from the gospels, sir."

"I don't understand you, my daughter."

" There is so much charity, monseigneur, so
much love, in the gospels."

" To be sure, to be sure! so there ought to
be. The Church sanctions charity; she always
has done so. But we must not be weak! We
must not allow a false kindness to spare the
bodies of the heretics to the peril of their souls
and the souls of those who come in contact with
them."

" We shall never agree, Monsieur l'Abbé,
since Philippe and I cannot accept your distinction of human reason *versus* divine. The
Spirit, we think, bloweth where it listeth; not
always among the so-called faithful. Neither
can I believe that our Lord Jesus Christ would,
if He could have seen it feasible, have strangled
or annihilated those sceptical Jews who refused
to recognize His authority."

Marie opened her eyes very wide at this. It
sounded so blasphemous; and yet it sounded
at the same time so very plausible, that she
trembled almost with nervous expectation of
the abbé's reply.

But the sudden entrance of la Mère Gabrielle put an end to the discussion; and she,
not doubting that Philippe was a peasant-girl,
kissed him on the cheek, and expressed her joy

at his having found a safe asylum amongst them. Then came an awkward silence, during which each looked uneasily at the other, till the abbé rose and drew the Superior out of the chamber on some pretext. Then the three put their heads together and planned a brave scheme for escaping from St. Michel.

The sun was dipping his disc, red and swollen out of all proportions, into the western waves, when the boy, kissing his sister for the last time, stole down the steps of the monastery to the narrow court below, and, avoiding the group of gesticulating pilgrims in the front of the hostelry, sought admittance at a side door, and threw himself with a cry of delight in the arms of his friend, who had grown as nervous as a young mother about Philippe's long absence, although Lisette had been up to the monastery twice and reported "all well." But Henri loved Philippe for Marie's sake.

CHAPTER XV.

THERE was tapping against the bedroom walls of the chamber occupied by Henri and Philippe, there were cries from angry pilgrims of " Hold your tongue!" and " Go to sleep!" as the murmur of Philippe's voice continued far into the night, broken by the deeper tones of his companion's questioning. How she looked ? what she said ? would she consent to fly ? and a thousand other queries were put and answered. But Henri could not sleep that night; there was something of reserve in Philippe's manner when he spoke of his sister's regard for him that awakened his suspicions. " She is changed in some sort—I know not why," Philippe had said ; and the meditative sadness that hung like an echo about his tone seemed to suggest more than his mere words expressed.

Henri had been unable to see Marie this

time, except at a distance, when she was
pacing with the old sisters to the *tierce* or
sexte, and so well disguised was he in the garb
of an apothecary, that Marie had not recognzied
him. He had paid the sacristan for permission
to accompany that worthy in his rounds of in-
spection amongst the pinnacles and minarets of
the windy roof, or in the dusty belfry, where the
whirling martens flew in and out impatient of
their presence, or still better, on the *promenoir*
by the church, whence Marie would sometimes
gaze on the boundless expanse of sea and sand.
But fortune was unkind, and neither in silent
chapel nor on leaden parapet could he obtain a
glimpse of the little foot, or catch a note of the
mellow voice, of her for whom he yearned. He
had made friends with the cheery almoner,
who each morning doled out long strips of
bread to the aged and the infirm who jostled
at the gate of the monastery; but no Marie
came to see the distribution.

When, then, he lay awake on the hard pallet
bed, feeling that to-morrow they must be away
with the pilgrims, while their presence was still
unnoticed in the general throng, he brooded
over the future with little of hope in his breast.
But Sleep is a kindly god, and he knit up for

Henri the ravelled sleeve of care in about the space of six hours, for, starting up and rubbing his eyes, as the sound of the bell for matins came ringing through the mist of early morning, he cried—

" One more venture, Phil! I am going to matins, for I feel wondrously devout this morning." ·

And the boy murmured something in his sleep and turned over, for his sleeve of care was not to be knit up under eight hours ; and, indeed, more than once Lisette had chidden him into a drowsy consciousness long after the rest of the house was up and astir. And her chiding had been all the more vigorous, perhaps, to make up for the stolen kiss with which she had sucked the honey of his breath, as he lay, child-like, pressing one rosy cheek upon the crumpled pillow. So she kissed first and scolded afterwards, thereby saving appearances.

And Henri, donning his large cloak and broad-brimmed hat, strode up to the abbey-church with a vague hope of meeting Marie. As usual, there were a few Benedictines in the choir, two or three of the sisters in their grated hiding-place, one or two old women kneeling in the nave, whom the coming dole had enticed thus early from their hovels. The sacristan nodded familiarly to Henri as he passed up the church, the precentor sent one of the choristers to him with a book of the chaunts, the prior's chaplain waited until he had taken his seat. The ex-lieutenant began to feel himself quite at home, almost ecclesiastical in himself; he sang with the loudest, and almost blushed, when the black, ill-shaven precentor at the end of the psalm made Henri a slight bow in acknowledgment of his vocal assistance. Then came the end of the service, and Henri stood up as the prior and the monks went out in procession through a side-chapel. He, too, was turning to depart, when a shuffle of hurried feet, an indecorous talking in the sacred building, arrested him for a moment, and immediately the grave-faced sub-prior came striding rapidly down the church towards him.

"Monsieur is an apothecary, I believe?"

Henri bowed.

"Unfortunately one of the sisters has fainted; the barber-surgeon is away, will monsieur kindly lend his help?"

Henri bowed again, and followed the sub-prior with an air half-amused, half-puzzled. For killing, not curing, had been his trade.

However, in those days the distinction was not much more than verbal.

The sub-prior led him to the door of a little cell, where stood Aunt Justine in her night-cap and slippers. Henri removed his hat with reluctance, fearing he should now be discovered; but he trusted to his good brown peruke to avert discovery.

"Vite, monsieur!" cried Aunt Justine, "my niece is taken with a fainting fit."

"Thank God!" murmured Henri, unconsciously uttering his thoughts.

"Hé quoi!" cried the spinster.

"Thank God, madame, it is only a faint." .

"Bad enough, monsieur, in all conscience. This comes of your papistical services at untimely hours—a judgment, I say!"

Henri put his hand on the little wrist, where the pulse was timorously fluttering. He stroked back the long brown hair which had fallen over Marie's pale brow; the long eyelashes almost brushed her cheeks.

Whilst the attendants were preparing, by the apothecary's directions, a burnt feather, Henri was wondering how he could get rid of the troublesome old aunt, who at any time, he feared, might recognize him. Two sisters were

supporting Marie in their arms on a couch;
Aunt Justine was still standing in the doorway,
trying to conceal her nightcap under a shawl.
Suddenly the apothecary started up and exclaimed—

"Madame, are you not well? do you feel a
spasm here?" touching her left side.

"Non, monsieur."

"Then you will shortly; I detect the presence of heart disease. Lose no time, madame,
in going back to bed; this excitement is full of
danger."

Aunt Justine put her hand hastily to her side,
and detected what the apothecary had pre-
dicted—an affection, or affectation, of the heart!

"Some one carry me to my bed!" she cried,
staggering under the idea of the agony which
should have accompanied her malady. And as
one of the old nuns lent her a helping arm,
Aunt Justine climbed faltering down the stone-
staircase, murmuring to herself, in a half-
reproachful tone, "Broken in pieces like a
potter's vessel!"

Henri was now left alone with Marie and
the other nun.

"Has the demoiselle no friend of her own
age?" he inquired, gravely tapping a tortoise-

shell snuff-box which he held in his left hand.
"Then summon her immediately, if you please."

Henri was now left alone with Marie and
opportunity. He bent over her, called her by
name, rubbed her hands, supported her drooping head; but do what he would, he could not
recall to consciousness the swooning girl. The
precious moments were fleeting, moments that
might turn the current of his life's history this
way or that. How beautiful she looked, this
fallen lily! how milky white the cheeks that he
dare not touch, though there was no flashing
eye to guard their purity; how graceful were
the lines of her slender, shapely form; how
sweetly the parted lips revealed the glimmer of
a string of pearls! What would he not have
given for those eye-lashes, which only a Van-
dyke could have painted, to rise and let him
bathe in the crystal of the liquid eyes they
veiled! "Marie! ma mie! ma mignonne!" No!
it was all in vain! a figure of wax would
have counterfeited life better. And now came
tripping feet up the staircase; "Ah! voici
l'Anglaise!" thought Henri, remembering the
boy-like agility of Marie's friend.

"Comment! you alone, Monsieur le Médecin,
with mademoiselle!"

"Oui, Mademoiselle Ethel, mais vous voyez un médecin malgré lui!"

"Est-ce Henri? Ma foi! how came you hither?" Then, observing Marie lying senseless on the couch, "Ah! cold water! quick!"

And before Henri could answer, she was out of the chamber again.

And the *médecin malgré lui* began rubbing and kissing his patient's hands with fresh vigour, looking all the time very much reconciled to the disagreeable situation in which chance had placed him.

Back came Ethel with a ewer of water, which she and Henri sprinkled plentifully on the reposeful face, until a sob burst from the throat and lungs, and the breath of life was quickened anew, though still the brain was held spell-bound and unthinking in the frozen winter that suspended circulation had created in its wondrous involutions.

"To-morrow night," whispered Henri, "a boat will be waiting at Tombelaine. When the moon rises above the cathedral of Avranches, quit the abbey; Gustave will show you your way. It will be high tide—he will row you to yon rock—the frigate is in the offing. Did she stir?"

" Her bosom heaved—she is still unconscious,
but her pulse is stronger. I will tell her your
plans. We will not disappoint you ; I have got
all ready for a sudden flight. I hear steps ;
have you any other message ? "

" Oui, oui, tell her how fondly I love her,
how my life is at her service ! Tell her I regret
the hasty words that I spoke in the dormitory.
Ethel, if my heart were opened, one deep,
engrossing love would be found sculptured
there, one name only, my darling's !—mine, if
not in this world, yet in the life to be ! "

As the lover uttered these passionate words,
Ethel had fixed her eyes upon his ; when he
ceased, she looked down and started at seeing
the dark grey eyes of Marie wide open, glistening, intelligent ! But though intelligent, there
was no happiness kindling them into laughter.
Calmly, but sadly, they regarded the two figures
standing by her couch, for the last words
spoken had entered her brain like fiery shafts ;
inwardly she was burning with the fever of
jealousy, outwardly she displayed the studied
calmness of despair. And just when Henri
was going to take her hand and say the words
that would have brushed away every cobweb
of suspicion and smoothed the path of love,

the Lady-Abbess of Fontevraud stood in the doorway. Making a formal courtesy to the pretended apothecary, she gave him pretty plainly to understand that his services were no longer required—

"You will please to ask Father Petre for your fee," she added, and bowed him incontinently out of the chamber before he could exchange a glance with Marie.

"My daughters," said the abbess, "who could have been so ill-advised as to introduce that man into our private apartments, even though poor Marie did seem to need medical skill? I confess that the loose discipline which prevails at Mont St. Michel almost makes me tremble. To be sure, the nuns here are old women, and only occupy these apartments as a species of almshouse; but when young girls like you two are exposed to such accidents as this, however innocent the facts may really be, I cannot but think that we are opening the door for scandal to walk in. I intend to beg Bishop Claude's permission to take you both to Fontevraud; I trust I shall be doing what is agreeable to your wishes."

Marie sat up and thanked Sister Gabrielle in a low voice. Ethel said nothing.

"I wish you were of us!" said the abbess, putting her arm round Ethel's waist.

"As I am not, it would be useless to trouble you with my company. Marie, too, needs me no longer; I will seek my fortunes elsewhere. Marie shall go her way, and I mine."

Marie choked down a bitter retort, and answered sadly—

"Since friendship is so frail a thing, let us part before events occur which may make us think worse of each other."

Ethel stared in blank astonishment, nor could she read the riddle that was written on her friend's contracted brow. The abbess looked at both silently, then observed to herself—

"They have quarrelled!"

"What did you mean, ma chère?" said Ethel, when they were left together.

"Ask your own heart; do not pretend to be so innocent."

"My heart tells me nothing that can account for your strange manner towards me, Marie, neither can I divine why you seem so sad. Henri bade me say——"

"Hush! tell me no more! Never repeat that name to me again, lest I loathe it in your presence. He was an atheist once; I tutored myself to surrender him. He pretended he had found peace at last in religion, but he was anchoring in the miasma of unfaith after all. And now I will hear of him no more, not though my father call him friend a thousand times, not though you go on your knees to me."

Ethel sighed and shook her head. Had she been better versed in love-making, she would have detected her friend's fatal mistake at once. But she was so frank and simple herself, and there were no novels in those days to poison young girls' minds with suggestions to sin, and so she put it down to Henri's avowal that he would never wed with a Papist, said no more, and trusted that the wound would heal in time. And when she disclosed the scheme of taking flight on the morrow, she had some trouble to persuade Marie to consent to it, and only succeeded by showing her that Henri had no part in it, and that Philippe would be anxiously awaiting their arrival at Tombelaine; that to refuse to flee would probably bring the boy back to St. Michel, and put his life once more in jeopardy.

And Henri went back to the hostelry, where he found Philippe sitting up in bed and reading a letter. The boy threw it to him as he entered.

"Lisez, mon cher, it is written for you as much as for me."

And Henri went to the dusty window and read the sieur's letter, newly come :—

"MY DEAR SONS—

"As I must now consider you both—I can only send you a few lines, for our captain drills us so frequently in rowing and manœuvring, that there is little leisure and less daylight for scribbling. I am still at the oar, and, indeed, begin to feel quite reconciled to my task ; the chief drawback is the foul language which certain of the criminal class make use of. Poor La Rose is dead ; the bastinado weakened him, and he never rallied enough to bear the fatigue and exposure of the ensuing nights of frost or rain. For myself, as I lie huddled up in my cloak upon the bench, watching the moon-beams glinting on the moving waves, or looking up at some gentle-eyed star that twinkles in the grand empurpled dome of heaven, I feel supremely happy—chained in body, yet free in spirit ; for they cannot curb the impetuous flight of thought, they cannot prevent me from mounting to the throne of the Unseen, from holding communion with the Father of all ·

Mercies. And God is very good to me; He fills my soul with joy and gladness, my heart with thanksgiving! I declare to you I never knew happiness till now, never felt so keenly the love of Christ, never received such celestial comfort, such holy peace, such a sense of suffering with God and for God. And I have been mightily upborne by reading Arrian's 'Fragments of Epictetus,' lent me by a learned gentleman chained on the next bench for passing the frontiers without a passport.

"Sometimes I have thought, What good do I in resisting his Majesty, being but a single person? Hear what Epictetus says: 'What good does the purple do on the garment? Why, it is splendid in itself, and splendid also in the example which it affords.' My sons, the chaplain has assured me that I may have my liberty if I will abjure; but as the spirit excelleth the body, so far is it better to lie in bonds for the truth than to enslave the soul for the sake of liberty to move the mere limbs of one. As Socrates nobly saith, 'Anytus and Melitus can indeed slay me, but harm me they cannot.' And again with Epictetus, 'I believe that God does all things well, and so need never murmur or complain.' And now, my sons, I leave you with one motto, 'Sustine et abstine'—bear what God assigns you, and forbear from evil. And, thinking of me, pray for me as I pray for you, that we may do God's will on earth, and ever willingly cry, 'God's will be done!'

"We are some of us to go to Paris soon, I hear, and then to the south. I would Marie were safe with my cousin, the Baron de Salgas. I have another letter from him, giving in detail a shorter route, which I enclose—utere quo vis —but have him strictly informed of your arrangements. The men of our Religion are very strong in the Cevennes; none dare oppose them. It would give me pleasure to think that my dear ones were still near me, and Languedoc is still France. Farewell!"

"Your father has an unbroken spirit, Philippe. I love the brave good man!"

Philippe's eyes were wet with tears.

"And here I lie in bed," he exclaimed, "while my father suffers in the chill air. Were it not for Marie, I swear I would give myself up and go to the galleys too!"

END OF VOL. II.

www.ingramcontent.com/pod-product-compliance
Lightning Source LLC
Chambersburg PA
CBHW060556030726
47498CB00005B/1419